The Secrets of the Underland

The Secrets
of the
Underland

A Drabek-Prime

Matador
9 Priory Business Park,
Wistow Road, Kibworth Beauchamp,
Leicestershire. LE8 0RX
Tel: 0116 279 2299
Email: books@troubador.co.uk
Web: www.troubador.co.uk/matador
Twitter: @matadorbooks

ISBN 978 1838593 803

British Library Cataloguing in Publication Data.
A catalogue record for this book is available from the British Library.

Printed and bound in the UK by TJ International, Padstow, CornwallTypeset in 11pt
Minion Pro by Troubador Publishing Ltd, Leicester, UK

Matador is an imprint of Troubador Publishing Ltd

For Tomasz and Amelka

Chapter One

A New Life

Timber woke with a nagging feeling that there was something important that he should have remembered, but he couldn't think what it was. He looked up at the window and felt the rays of the sun cascading through the glass straight onto his face. He stretched out his limbs to each corner of the bed and tried to shake off the fact that he could really do with another few hours' sleep. As he relaxed back down into the comfort of his duvet, he smiled to himself about the day ahead. It was a lovely September morning and he had just started Year 5 in his new school. At the beginning of the summer he'd moved with his parents to a new house in a new city. His dad got a new job at the local university and his mum had just opened a new hairdressing salon. He'd been worried about how the move would go, but he really liked his new room in the new house, and the boys at school were much nicer than the boys in his old one. The girls were nicer too. Everything seemed to be much nicer here. His parents were very excited about the move and they seemed to enjoy the new place as much as he did.

Tim jumped out of bed and went to the bathroom to brush his teeth and comb his hair, which was a very difficult thing to do because his hair had always had a life of its own. It stuck out in places and no matter what he did, it always looked like he'd just got out of bed. It was slightly curly, and Tim always thought he could lose a lot of toys in its midst. It actually happened once that he was walking around with two pencils hidden in his hair... it was two days before he discovered them during his weekly hair-washing session. His mum loved his hair, and she was the only person who could just about get it under control. And so she did, when Tim appeared for breakfast.

"How is my favourite boy today?" she asked with a smile.

"I'm fine," yawned Tim into his bowl of cornflakes. "Where's Dad?"

"He had to go to work early today to prepare himself before the students come back for the new term, and there was some trouble in the lab during the night which he's got to sort out."

"What trouble?" asked Tim curiously.

"I don't know; but I'm sure he'll tell us when he comes home. Now, eat your cereal or you'll be late for school," his mum said firmly before leaving the kitchen to finish getting ready for work. "Do you need a lift to school?" she called from the hall.

"No, thanks. I'll walk."

"OK; see you later, sweetheart. I love you," she called as she walked upstairs.

Tim enjoyed the freedom of walking to school all by himself. It made him feel older and more responsible. Just old enough to suit his name – Timber; his mum invented it and he absolutely detested it. He was grateful he could shorten it to something normal! He'd had a lot of trouble with boys at his old school because of his wretched name, and he quickly got used to introducing himself as Tim instead. He didn't mind his new friends calling him that. He didn't mind it because they didn't do it in a nasty manner like the boys from his old school. But now he just wanted to forget about his old life. It was a difficult and not very pleasant one. He had a chance for a new start now and he was planning to grab that chance with both hands.

It was a truly beautiful morning. Tim could feel the warmth of the sun on his back as he walked the picturesque route to school. He only had to cross one road and it wasn't a very busy one. He noticed the leaves delicately falling from their branches. He caught a red one and lifted it to the sun. The wonderful red glow softly touched his eyes. He closed them and imagined that he was the captain of a big spaceship flying into space. He and his crew were exploring new ways to travel and he was well known and loved by everybody, and—

"Hi, what are you doing?" A girl's voice brought him back from the sky and he opened his eyes.

"Err… hi," he said shyly.

She was as small as him and Tim could see a hint of maroon peeking out from her coat, which suggested she was in the same school as he was. She looked straight into his eyes with her huge green ones. She had a lovely round face and red hair gathered in a ponytail at the back of her head. She smiled a truly genuine smile that made her cheeks bulge, and it made Tim feel slightly less embarrassed that he'd been caught daydreaming.

"What are you doing?" she repeated without any hint of annoyance in her voice.

Tim wasn't used to people talking to him, especially girls; unless they were annoyed at him, of course. He didn't know what to say.

"Err… I was just, err… nothing!" He wanted to turn around and run away, but he felt like he was glued to the ground, pinned down by her jewel-like green eyes.

"It didn't look like nothing to me. It looked like you were far, far away. What's your name?"

"Timber Green," he blurted out. "I mean, Tim."

"Hi, Timber Green I Mean Tim, I'm Molly." She smiled again and even though she'd mocked him, her smile was still bursting with kindness; not a hint of viciousness or menace. Tim liked her smile and he wasn't quite sure why, but he knew he liked her too.

"I saw you yesterday," said Molly, "you're the new boy from 5F. I'm in 5B."

"Hi…" Suddenly Tim felt so silly; he just didn't know what to say to her. His mind was blank, and every word he'd ever known had just vanished from his head. He just wanted to disappear, just go straight underground and never appear again.

"If we stand here any longer, we'll be late for school," Molly said, putting an end to the awkward silence. "Do you want to walk together?"

"Yeah…" He felt brainless.

So they walked in silence – Molly with a smile on her face, Tim with a sick feeling in his stomach.

"If I see you after school, we can walk home together," said Molly when they reached the school gate.

"Err… yeah…" managed Tim. *Oh goodness, she must think I'm a cave boy*, he thought, embarrassed beyond belief.

Molly smiled, blushing a little herself, and ran for the door to her classroom.

"Good morning, Timber," he heard just behind him. It was Mrs Julius, the head teacher. "How was your first day at school yesterday?"

"It was good, thank you, Mrs Julius," Timber replied, relieved he'd found the power of speech again.

"Well, I hope today will be equally good. Now run along or you'll miss the register."

Timber made it to registration with seconds to spare, and the rest of the school day went without incident, which was a rarity for him. He got to know a few boys and played with them at lunch and break. For the first time ever, it felt like school was a place he actually wanted to be. His teacher, Mrs Long, was very nice too. She smiled a lot and didn't shout at children like the teacher in his old school. He couldn't believe it; everything was better here than at the old school.

After lunch they had playtime in the school gardens. Tim and his new-found friends decided to play hide and seek, and he found a perfect spot to hide behind the flowerbed, next to the school wall. Nobody could see him there because the flowers created a perfect hiding place and covered him from all sides. He could stand up straight, and if he parted the leaves he could see the playground and the other boys running around frantically trying to find him. *They'll never find me here*, he thought.

He stood there for some time, but then he started to get bored. *Maybe I hid too well*, he thought. *Maybe I should make some noise...* He didn't want to just leave his perfect hiding place, so he thought the noise idea was a touch of genius. He stood still for a moment to think about how he could make a noise in the flowerbed without being too obvious, and that was when he heard it...

"*Hello, is anybody there?*" Tim stood stock still and listened. "*Grump, is that you? Hello?!*"

Tim could swear that the voice was coming from underneath him. But how could that be possible – he was standing on the flowerbed – there wasn't any 'underneath' here. Then he thought that maybe the other boys were playing a trick on him. He jumped out from behind the flowers with a loud, "Boo!" But there was nobody there. What's more, he noticed that the lunch break was over and all the other children had gone indoors. Not wanting to get into trouble in his first week, he ran to his classroom and apologised for being late.

"Where have you been?" asked Thomas. "We couldn't find you anywhere."

"Boys, you have to be quiet now," said Mrs Long. The boys smiled at each other and then turned their attention to their teacher. Tim really wanted to share with them what he'd heard, but he was worried they'd think he was crazy if he told them, so he decided to keep quiet.

The afternoon went so quickly that Tim didn't even notice that it was already home time. He met Molly at the school gate as she'd suggested. He still felt very nervous but slightly less than he had that morning.

"How was your day?" asked Molly.

"It was interesting."

"Oh my goodness, you can really talk," said Molly cheekily; they both burst into laughter.

From that moment the conversation just seemed to flow and Timber really opened up to her. He told her about his old school and about all the nasty things the other boys did and said to him. Then he told her how much happier he felt in the new place.

"Everything is better here: our new house, new school, new children. I feel I can make friends… and even my name doesn't sound like an insult anymore."

The pair walked and talked all the way to Timber's front door, and as they said their goodbyes, Tim realised that he was very lucky that Molly approached him that morning and he knew that she was going to be his friend. She already was.

Chapter Two

Mysterious Whispers and How To Keep A Secret

The next morning Tim couldn't wait to see Molly again. She was his first real friend, a person who didn't laugh at him, was kind, sincere and also interesting to talk to. They met on the way to school again, and this time Tim was a bit more articulate than yesterday.

"Hi Molly," he said with a big smile on his face.

"Hi!"

They walked for some time in silence, but it wasn't awkward; in fact Tim found it quite comfortable.

"What are you up to after school?" Molly asked as they neared the school gate.

"Not much today; I have to go straight home because

my mum needs to drop off some things at my dad's office and I promised to go with her. How about you?"

"My mum's taking me out of school early today – I've got to go to the dentist." Molly grimaced. But her grimace was soon replaced with her trademark face-filling smile. "It's my birthday on Saturday; will you come to my party?"

"Yeah, I'd love to," said Tim, and his eyes widened with delight. "Where is it?"

"I'll give you an invitation tomorrow morning. It's at my house," replied Molly with a big grin.

At the school gates they said their goodbyes and ran to their classrooms.

At lunchtime the boys were playing hide and seek again, and Tim decided to use yesterday's hideout since it hadn't been discovered. It had rained in the night, so the soil was all soggy and the leaves were still wet. He could feel his wellies sinking deeper and deeper into the soil but didn't want to move too much in case one of the boys was nearby. It was then, when he was breathing quietly and standing motionless to avoid being heard by the others, that he heard the whispering voice again.

"*Hello, is anybody there?*"

Tim stood frozen to the ground. He'd forgotten all about yesterday's adventure.

"*Grump, is that you? Hello?! Please answer me, Grump.*"

Tim was sure now that the voice was coming from underneath him. But how could that even be possible? He was standing in the flowerbed, in the middle of the day, in his ordinary school playground. In all his life nothing out of the ordinary had ever happened to him. *There must be a logical explanation to all those whispers*, thought Tim. *And who is Grump?!* He scratched his head and then it came to him. *There must be somebody hidden on the other side of the wall, playing jokes on me and trying to scare me*, he thought. *Yes, that's it*, thought Tim, *I bet the boys saw me hiding here and decided to play a little game on me.*

He pushed his way between the wall and the plants and jumped out just at the corner of the school wall to catch them in the act. There was nobody there. Well, it was lunchtime, so there were a lot of kids running around, but there was nobody there behind the wall of his school, nobody who could make those whispers. So where did they come from? He looked back warily; he wasn't sure he was brave enough to go there again. Instead he headed back to his classroom, had something to drink and decided to wait there for his friends. They soon came running inside and the afternoon's lessons started. Tim wanted to tell somebody about what he'd heard, but he wasn't sure how the boys would react to it. He didn't want anybody to laugh at him again. He really liked it here and he feared that telling his story may change things between him and the boys. If there was only somebody he could trust, one friend to share things with, one person who wouldn't laugh, who would believe him. And then the obvious solution unravelled itself in his head... Molly! He'd tell her tomorrow.

*

The creature woke up when the boy jumped out from behind the flowerbed. He had seen him here yesterday. The boy was the reason behind his failed attempt to communicate with Grug, and Grump really detested the vile being. He didn't like humans in general. Their world was full of weirdness and danger, although he had to admit it was also a world filled with wonder, and in Grump's opinion humans didn't deserve to live there. Hogmills, on the other hand, were the proper creatures to master this world. He wished Grug could be here with him. He was his brother and best friend. They grew up together and were inseparable from a very young age. Truth be told, this was the first time that they'd ever separated from each other, and Grump didn't like it one bit. He couldn't understand how it was even possible for him to end up in the human world. The last thing he could remember was the two of them in the tunnels, talking and joking. Grug was supposed to show him the mysterious object he had found in one of the smaller tunnels, when suddenly he got sucked up by an immense gust of wind and ended up on the cold flowerbed covered in mud.

That was a few nights ago now; nights that he had to spend on the cold ground waiting for whispers from his brother. He could hear him but didn't know how to answer. He tried shouting, whispering back, he dug the soil with his bare hands, but nothing seemed to help – he could hear Grug, but Grug couldn't hear him. Grump was beginning to think that he would be stuck there forever without his brother and friend, and for him that was the most horrible thought imaginable. It had only been a few days, but Grump had absolutely had enough of this world already. Any world without his best friend just wouldn't do, but here, with constant rain at night, and the soggy mud making his lovely coat a hideous grey colour, it didn't help ease his homesickness. And on top of all that, he had humans and their loud offspring to worry about. Grump just couldn't figure them out. He hadn't been bothered much in this secluded piece of garden, until that boy showed up, of course. Not only had he spoiled Grump's attempts at communication with Grug, but what was worse, he had heard Grug's whispers, and now Grump was facing the very real danger that grown-up humans might show up and investigate his hiding place. He feared he hadn't much time left. He needed to find his way back home and he needed to do so very soon.

*

The afternoon flew by in a haze of spelling tests and fractions, and Tim rushed home to help his mum. They went to his dad's office and then all three of them went out for dinner. It was their first meal out since they'd moved here.

"To our first family meal," his dad said, raising his glass, "to celebrate new beginnings."

When the waiter brought the pizza, Tim almost fell off his chair. It was the largest one he had ever seen. It was followed by a colossal mound of sugary goodness and the flavours that exploded in Tim's mouth took his mind away from anything that had happened that afternoon. The mysterious whispers slipped right to the back of his mind. It was a proper family night out, with jokes, lots of laughter and not getting back home till way past Tim's usual bedtime. It was a school night, so he had to go straight to bed as soon as he stepped through the front door. As his head hit the pillow he began to think about the next day… he couldn't wait to see Molly. He needed to tell her about the mysterious whispers and maybe together they could play detectives and investigate the strange occurrence in their school playground.

*

Molly wasn't at their usual meeting point the next morning. Tim felt a wave of sadness and disappointment, and to his surprise, he almost burst into tears. He remembered that yesterday she was supposed to go to the dentist, but that's all. He hoped she was all right. He was almost at the school gates when he heard his name being called. He turned around and saw Molly running up the path. His pulse quickened in joy.

"Molly, where have you been?"

"We overslept today – total rush this morning. I can't believe I'm on time!" She stood next to Tim, slightly bent over to catch her breath.

"Have you run all the way?"

"Yes, I wanted to give you this," and she pulled something from her bag and handed it to Tim.

"What is it?" asked Tim, at the same time ripping into the paper envelope.

"It's my birthday party invitation; it's only two days from now. Will you come?"

"Of course I will," said Tim happily. Then he realised that he still hadn't told Molly anything about the strange whispers. Well, they didn't have any time left now, so they arranged a meeting after lunch – he could tell her and show her the place at the same time.

The morning dragged dreadfully. He couldn't concentrate on anything. He was told off twice for daydreaming and he forgot which way to run during PE games and lost his team a few points. Ordinarily he'd be stressing that the others would be annoyed with him, but he couldn't care less today; he just wanted lunchtime to arrive and put him out of his madness of anticipation. At last the bell rang.

He met Molly and they walked to the quietest place in the playground.

"You're definitely being very mysterious today, Tim. What's going on?"

"I need to tell you something, but you need to promise me first that you're not going to laugh at me." Tim was starting to get very nervous; what if he was wrong about Molly and she was going to laugh at him or, what's more, she wouldn't believe him? But he couldn't back away now; he had to tell her whatever the outcome.

"Yesterday, and the day before as well, I heard mysterious whispers in the playground…" Tim proceeded to tell her all about his hiding place and what he had heard and how there was nobody to blame it on. When he finished, she didn't laugh, she just stared at him with her huge green eyes.

"Who do you think it was?" Molly asked.

"I have no idea. It sounded like it was coming from underground and at the same time from very far away."

"Hmm, there's no basement at school," thought Molly aloud, "and anyway, I don't think you could have heard whispers from the basement even if we had one. What was the name the whisperer called again?"

"Grump, whoever that is," said Tim. "Do you want me to show you where I heard it?"

"Yes, please," said Molly. She hesitated for a second. "I'm a little bit scared, Tim."

"Don't worry, there's lots of people in the playground and we can always call for help. Do you want me to hold your hand?" Tim was feeling really brave now.

Molly felt reassured by his bravery and they strode across the playground together. Then, hand in hand, they disappeared behind the flowerbed to investigate the mystery.

*

Grump was munching on an apple which he had found earlier that day when he heard the voices of approaching children.

I knew it, he thought, *I knew that boy couldn't keep quiet and now he's brought trouble with him.*

Grump hid deeper in the bushes so he was invisible, but at the same time he could see the children very clearly. The boy – *wretched thing* – had brought a girl with him this time. They were standing on the spot where Grug's whispers were the most audible. Oh, how much Grump wished for silence from the ground. Maybe if they would hear nothing they would go away and never come back again. Then his secret would be safe and he could concentrate his efforts on finding his way back home, not hiding away from human offspring. He was getting really angry, but he had no idea what to do. The children were holding hands and looking around with visible fear on their faces.

"Can you hear anything?" asked the girl.

"No," answered the boy, "maybe I just imagined I could hear something."

Yes, that's a good line of thinking. Grump smiled to himself. Maybe there was a chance that they would go away after all.

"I think we should stand here quietly and listen for a moment. Maybe we have to be in complete silence to hear him," said the girl. "Anyway, whatever happens I think we should keep it a secret, what do you think, Tim?"

No, no, no! Grump almost shouted in his head. *Go away, you evil things, go away!*

"Maybe you're right, Molly. Let's do that." So they stood quietly for some time, but the only thing they heard was the bell announcing the end of lunch break and the beginning of the afternoon classes. Disappointed and still holding hands, the children left the flowerbed and a very angry Grump behind.

Chapter Three

Missing Hair Clip and How To Get Under

"What do you think, Molly?" asked Tim.

"I don't know what to think," Molly replied thoughtfully. "I believe that you've heard something, but I think it may have been an echo of somebody talking on the playground. You know a travelling sound or something."

Tim nodded in agreement. "Maybe you're right. Maybe I'm just being silly."

"No, you're not silly," she said, not wanting her friend to feel bad. "I still think we should investigate it further. We can talk about it on the way home."

"That's a good idea, but I have to go home straight after school. I've told my mum about your party invitation and we're going to get your birthday present."

Molly beamed coyly. "I'll see you at the gate."

The afternoon flew by and the children met by the gate as they said they would. Molly still looked rather thoughtful.

"What's up?" asked Tim.

"I lost my hair clip. I think it may have happened when we were in the flowerbed. I need to go and check."

"I'm sorry, Molly, but I promised my mum I'd be back straight after school."

"That's fine, don't worry. You go home; I'll check by myself and I'll tell you tomorrow morning if I hear anything there."

"Are you sure?" Tim said, amazed that Molly was being so brave.

"Of course I am. What could possibly happen to me? A little bit of mud on my shoes?" She chuckled.

"You're right. Those whispers have really messed with my head," Tim replied, embarrassed by his reaction to the whole thing. Molly was right; it was probably just an echo. "Beware of non-existing whispering monsters, O brave knightess Molly."

"Brave knightess, thank you very much – princess, maybe; but I'd rather be a ballerina, not a knight," said Molly, laughing out loud.

"OK, OK," agreed Tim, "go on then and dance in the mud or maybe jump in the muddy puddles, Peppa."

"Have you really just compared me to Peppa Pig?" shouted Molly with laughter.

"You said the pig word, not me," shouted Tim, running out of the gates and laughing hard.

"Ha, ha, I can't believe you've just said that! I'll get you tomorrow for that, Tim," Molly shouted back at him.

They waved at each other and turned to go, each in their own direction.

I'm so lucky to have such a good friend, thought Tim, *very lucky, indeed.*

*

Grump was furious when he saw the girl coming back. She squeezed through the bushes and started looking for something on the ground. *I'll teach you a lesson, you nosy thing*, he thought mischievously. Then he had an idea. He was going to scare her really badly, and after that she would never come back again. *And maybe she would tell that boy and they would keep away from now on*, thought Grump with a triumphant smile. He took as much air as he could into his lungs and, making a growling sound deep inside his throat, he ran straight for Molly.

*

Molly was still thinking of muddy puddles, laughing inwardly as she squeezed through the bushes. She couldn't see her clip anywhere. Suddenly she heard the rustling of leaves and then a weird growling sound. She thought that Tim had decided to come back to scare her after all. She smiled slightly with her eyes still on the ground... and in that exact moment she felt it – the strange gust of wind coming from underneath her feet. It was very strange because she could feel that wind under her feet, deep inside herself and all around her at the same time. She felt slightly dizzy and unsure on her feet. She lifted up her eyes and saw a strange creature charging in her direction. She didn't even have time to get scared. She felt herself falling, and then she saw nothing.

*

Grump ran with all his might. He saw the girl lifting her head and looking straight at him. She was so pretty, it almost stopped him in his tracks. He leapt and saw the expression on the girl's face change. She didn't look scared, though, it was more like awe that he could see on her face, and then she started falling. *What's going on?* Grump thought. He landed with a squashy sound in the mud. The girl was gone.

Chapter Four

Slith

It was one of the most brilliant ideas he had ever had. Now he was lying on the ground and pressing his face into the mud so he wouldn't burst into laughter. *Clever me*, he thought, *clever me*. He needed to go back to his master, but the look on this creature's face was too priceless for Slith to move on with his tasks. *Slith made him look like that, Slith did. Clever Slith*, he thought.

You may not know it, but Slith was the reason behind Grump's disappearance from his world. It wasn't intentional; it couldn't have been, because Slith wasn't intelligent at all. You see, he was a worm, and all his life was spent worming around in the ground until Master changed him. Now Slith, although still with a very small head and almost non-existent brain, was something else, something he was very proud of – a wriggling mass of slithery cunning. He thought of himself as a snake, but in reality he was still just a worm, a changed one, but still a worm. That was his master's cruel joke, but Slith couldn't understand any of this. He was Master's messenger, and he felt really important in this role. He carried messages and little ingredients that his master needed for making potions and magical mists. Master was going to inhabit the human world, and Slith was going to help Master to achieve this goal. It was Master who showed Slith how to travel between worlds. It was Master who gave him the gift of invisibility. *This is why the silly hogmill didn't even know what hit him*, Slith laughed to himself. He had seen them walking through the tunnels. The fatter one had found the shimmering of the portal and wanted to share it with his friend, almost uncovering Master's master plan. But clever Slith had prevented it by pushing the tall one through the portal headfirst. Now he was stuck in the human world without any means of getting back. Slith had the key to the portal and only he knew how to use it; Master had shown him. Now he'd played another joke on the creature… he'd sent the girl through the portal and made the hogmill's coat all muddy and dirty again. Slith laughed, chewing a mouthful of soil. But time was running out and he had to begin his return journey. Master was very impatient and didn't like to be kept waiting too long. Slith wasn't very intelligent, but he knew one thing – making Master angry was a very dangerous thing to do, very dangerous indeed.

Chapter Five

The Forgetting Stone

Molly felt herself falling. She closed her eyes, waiting for the impact of hitting the ground, but nothing like that happened. At first she saw nothing, but then she could see a beautiful blue light all around her. She was falling faster and faster. Then the light disappeared and she was thrown onto a bed-like surface. Everything puffed up around her and she felt as though she'd landed on a hundred duvets and pillows. It didn't hurt at all, but it took her breath away for a few seconds. She breathed in the pink mist that came out of the pillows and she suddenly felt really tired. She closed her eyes and drifted off to sleep.

*

Grug was just about to go back to his village to refill his food sacks and confess his weird ordeal to his family, and to complain about the lack of progress in communication, when he suddenly saw a blue light shining in the tunnel. He ran back and his heart was lit up by hope and happiness. He thought that maybe Grump had found his way home and that the moment of reunion had come at last. But to his shock and absolute horror, it wasn't Grump he saw falling down towards him… it was a human, a girl – she fell down and hit the stone beneath. The stone puffed up in a very un-stony way and a pink mist completely covered her. Grug looked upwards, waiting for Grump to appear next, but he didn't come. The pink mist eased and Grug could get a good look at the girl. She lay motionless on the stone, seemingly asleep. Grug couldn't take his eyes off her. He thought her the most beautiful thing he had ever seen. She had long, red hair and such a sweet face. She looked so peaceful. Grug stretched out his arm and gently touched her face with his fingertips. Her skin was soft and warm. When he touched her, the girl opened her eyes; they were amazing – green and lake-like, deep and shining. Grug hadn't expected her to wake up with quite so much urgency and, taking him by surprise, Grug lost his balance and he stumbled to the floor.

*

Molly felt herself waking from a very deep sleep. She felt something on her cheek and opened her eyes. She saw a pair of honey-coloured eyes looking straight at her from the depths of a very hairy face. The creature stumbled backwards and fell to the floor. It was the strangest creature Molly had ever seen. His whole body was covered in a light brown fur. His hands were hairy too, and finished with human-like palms and fingers but still in a light brown coloration. His face was quite round, with a muzzle of a mouth and teeth sticking out and those beautiful eyes covered by fringe-like fur.

"Are you all right?" asked Molly.

"You're not afraid of me?" asked the bewildered creature.

"Why would I be? You look friendly enough to me… although a little peculiar, no offence. Besides, this is the best dream I have ever had," said Molly with a smile on her face.

"Humans are usually afraid of us. They call us devils," said the creature.

"Well, those humans must be very silly, whoever they are," said Molly. "What's your name?"

"I'm Grug. I'm a hogmill and I live in these tunnels," he replied proudly. "What's your name, little human girl?"

Molly sat up and thought for a moment. The answer to that question should've come to her instantly, but it didn't. She looked at her hands. They were very different to Grug's. She touched her face. She couldn't feel any hair and her skin was warm and soft.

"I'm not like you," said Molly.

"No, you're not. You're human. What's your name?" Grug started to worry that the girl must have hit her head on the stone a little bit too hard when she fell.

"My name is… My name… is…" Molly felt tears rolling slowly down her cheeks. "I can't remember." She didn't like this dream anymore, so she started to pinch herself to wake up. She pressed her eyes closed, counted to ten, pinched herself twice more, but when she opened her eyes again, nothing had changed. She was still in the tunnel, still sitting on the stone and the very concerned honey-coloured eyes were still looking back at her.

"Why can't I wake up?" she asked.

"Maybe because you're not dreaming," Grug answered very quietly. "I saw you falling down into my world. I am very real, and so is this world."

"Where are we?"

"Welcome to Underland." Grug smiled, stretching out his hands to convey the extent of his world.

"Underland? I've never heard of it."

"No, you wouldn't have. You're from a different world. We know about you and your world, but we're trying to keep ourselves secret." Grug's open and welcoming face now took on a far more sombre demeanour.

"Why?"

"We tried many generations ago to communicate with your kind, but most humans didn't understand us, they thought us devils and demons and all sorts of evil things. It was very hurtful, and we decided to come back to our world."

"You said *most* humans?"

"Yes, not everyone is the same."

"Well, thank goodness for that," said Molly with a smile. "What are we going to do now? Why can't I remember anything?"

"We need to go to Mama G, she'll sort you out," said Grug very seriously.

"Who's Mama G?" asked Molly.

"What do you mean, who is she? She's my mother, and she's the elder of our tribe."

"You have a tribe?"

"Of course I do. We all live in tribes. Don't you?" Grug kept discovering that humans were even weirder than he thought.

"I don't know," Molly said with concern. She was beginning to feel really worried now. "I can't remember."

"Mama G will help you. She's the wisest hogmill I've ever known."

"OK, let's go and meet Mama G then." Molly jumped gracefully from the stone and looked around. "Which way should we go?" There were three tunnels leading out of the tiny cave they were in.

"We'll take the North Tunnel," said Grug. "It's the shortest one and the most peaceful."

"What do you mean, peaceful? Aren't the others?"

"There may be other travellers in the other two tunnels, and I don't think it would be good if anybody else knows that you're here before Mama G can tell us what to do about it all."

Grug felt really confident about the meeting with Mama G, so Molly started to feel hopeful too. She'd be all right if his mum was anything like Grug; she'd actually begun to grow quite fond of the curious little creature.

"It's horribly dark in this tunnel." Molly stopped abruptly, looking into the darkness.

"Wait until we put the lanterns on. You'll see what a beautiful place it is."

Grug put his hand over an oval stone and murmured something that Molly couldn't hear. When he finished, the stone lit up with a beautiful and soft golden light, and then little veins of golden light shot out from it and travelled down the tunnel walls. It was an incredible sight, almost like the tunnel had come alive with golden blood pumping through its living veins. What Molly saw in front of her exceeded all her expectations. She imagined an earthy dark tunnel, dirty and cold, but in reality, she now stood in front of a wonder. The tunnel was tall enough for a grown-up man to stand in and very comfortable to walk through. It was carved in some sort of crystal that had a lovely orange glow, intensified by the golden light. Something that looked like tree roots hung from the tunnel's ceiling and swirled around like amazing garlands, all green and yellow. The floor was orange too and covered in a soft carpet of moss that made walking quiet and very easy underfoot.

"It is breath-taking," said Molly with a smile.

"We are master carvers," said Grug with pride. "There is no stone or surface that we cannot carve through. This is how we found your world and all the others. We are protectors of the tunnels, protectors of the way. We made all the tunnels and caves in this world and, legend says, in all the other worlds as well."

"You are not only carvers, Grug; you're artists as well. This tunnel is absolutely perfect," said Molly, looking around, struggling to take it all in.

Grug smiled, very pleased with himself and pleased at Molly's appreciation of their work. He walked into the tunnel and let Molly follow him. There was a long walk in front of them and he was genuinely worried about this beautiful girl that had put her trust in him. He really hoped Mama G could help them. He should have asked her for help a long time ago instead of trying to figure it all out for himself. He couldn't understand what was going on and how he could make things go back to the way they were. He feared that if Mama G didn't have an answer, then nobody would, and that meant that they were all doomed.

Chapter Six

How Not To Worry When You Do

It had been a day and a half since Molly went missing and Tim didn't know what to do with himself. He was so worried and he blamed himself. He was sure it had something to do with the whispers, but he really couldn't put his finger on it just yet. Yesterday, when Molly didn't come to school, he thought that maybe she had caught a cold and stayed at home. He went with his mum to buy her birthday present and he was really excited about the party. The day dragged without her, but he played with the boys and was hopeful that he'd get to see her the next day.

In the afternoon Mrs Julius, the head teacher, came to Tim's classroom and asked him to come with her. She took him to her office and as she pushed the creaking door open, he spotted the familiar sight of his mum's coat draped across the back of a chair. Following Mrs Julius's instructions, he stepped inside the office, previously unchartered territory for him, and sure enough, there sat his mum; her eyes barely raised to meet his as she dabbed her cheek with a scrunched-up tissue. *What on earth is going on?* Tim thought, but he couldn't quite say it out loud. Possibly because he had a feeling he didn't really want to know. He hadn't even noticed the policewoman stood formally in the corner of the room.

Tim looked at his mum and noticed that she'd had blotchy cheeks, the same cheeks she had when they left their last house… he felt a numbing feeling in the pit of his stomach and his hands started to shake. His mum got up from the chair and gave him a big hug. Usually this would reassure him, but today it almost made him crazy with worry. Then she took him to the chair next to hers; he hadn't even noticed it there until now. He sat down and his mum explained to him that his friend Molly didn't come back home yesterday afternoon and that the police would like to ask him about the last time he saw her, and if she had told him anything about her plans for the afternoon.

"What do you mean?" he asked, unable to take in what he'd just heard. "Are you saying she's run away? Has she been taken?" Tim could feel his heart pounding in his chest as he spoke. "She was just going home, that's what she said; well… she had to get her hair clip first, but then she was going straight home. Why wouldn't she go home?" he said, his eyes pleading with his mum for answers.

He told them everything he could remember about their last meeting, keeping the whispers out of the conversation, of course, and now as he walked to his mum's car, he couldn't stop going through it in his head. Luckily Mrs Julius had agreed with his mum that he should go straight home after their meeting. He was in a bit of a state and he didn't want to go back to his classroom. As she walked Tim and his mum to the main gate, Mrs Julius offered some professional help, should Tim need it. But he didn't need any professional help – well, maybe Special Forces-type professional help to find Molly and figure out what the whispers were about, but nothing else.

He didn't sleep very well that night and his mum wanted him to stay at home from school the next day too, but he couldn't. He knew what he had to do. He had to go back to the flowerbed and investigate. Molly went there to look for her hair clip; there must be a clue left behind somewhere. That was the last place she said she would be and that was the place he was going to check really thoroughly... whispers or not. She was his best friend and that was the least he could do for her. He told his mum that he was going to school and she reluctantly agreed to let him, but she didn't want him to walk to school by himself anymore and he could quite understand why. If something could happen to Molly, then something could happen to him. He shivered as he thought about it.

"I'll wait for you at the gate after school, sweetheart," said his mum, and squeezed Tim a little bit tighter than normal. Tim looked around to check if anybody saw this embarrassing display of affection. Luckily for him, nobody did, and Tim breathed a sigh of relief. *It was a good idea to get a lift home*, he thought. Now he just had to last until lunchtime and then he'd proceed with his investigation.

Grump felt horrible. He knew that the human girl was in his world now, and that unless she found Grug, her life would be in danger. He felt angry with himself; angry and helpless. He couldn't understand what could have gone wrong. He just wanted to scare her; he didn't mean for any of this to happen. He thought through the night about what he could do to help, and he realised that he needed the human boy to help him. He needed to make contact. He was worried about the boy's reaction when he saw him, but there was nothing else to do. He decided he'd wait until night and then he'd leave his safe hiding place and go to look for the boy. In that exact moment Grump heard the noise of approaching footsteps. He looked out and like a mirage, the boy was there. *Well, there's a stroke of luck*, he thought. He gathered all his courage and stepped out.

*

The lunch break was here at last. Tim finished his lunch as quickly as possible (he didn't have to eat it all, but it was his favourite – fish and chips; nobody leaves fish and chips!). He ran out to the playground, and with cunning he slipped past a teacher and rushed into the flowerbed unnoticed. With his eyes on the ground, he looked for Molly's hair clip. He heard a rustling of leaves in front of him and he lifted his head. He didn't expect to see what he saw. The creature looked back at him and Tim felt his legs giving way underneath him. He saw the blue sky and then darkness.

*

Grump was worried about the boy's reaction when he saw him. He expected that he might scream or run away, but he never thought about the boy fainting. That was upsetting. He didn't have much choice, though; he picked the boy up from the ground and took him deeper into the bushes. He put him down on the bed he had made for himself out of leaves and branches, and tried to wake him up.

*

Tim thought it was morning again and for those first few moments he was sure he was back at home in bed, and that his mum was going to come into his room any minute now to wake him up for school.

"Are you all right?" asked the voice. It wasn't his mum's, and as he slowly opened his eyes into something more than just slits, Tim suddenly remembered everything.

"Please don't eat me," was the only thing he could think of to say. His eyes were tightly shut again now, and his heart was racing in his chest.

"Now, why would I do that?" said Grump in a very hurt voice. He hadn't known what to expect, but he certainly hadn't expected a reaction like that. *Nothing has changed in this world*, he thought.

There was something in the creature's voice that made Tim dare to open his eyes and look at him. A kind of sadness and longing. *Evil creatures growl and snarl*, Tim thought, *they don't make you feel sorry for them.* Tim looked hard at the creature. He had lovely honey-coloured eyes, although Tim could see that they were very sad eyes. Tim looked the creature up and down; head to toe, he was a mass of dark brown fur, and he was taller than Tim too. Tim wondered whether that made him a small adult or a tall child.

"Who are you?" Tim asked, feeling a little bit braver.

"My name is Grump, I am a hogmill and I'm lost in your world."

OK, thought Tim, *I can deal with that.* "My name is Tim," he said, and put his hand out to Grump. "I am a human and this is my world… and I am very sorry for my earlier behaviour."

Grump smiled at that.

"You see, I'm a little bit worried, because my friend, Molly, has gone missing, and the last place she said she was going to be was here, and I've heard whispers, and—"

"I know where your friend is," said Grump.

"You do?" said Tim, not sure whether to be excited or worried for her safety.

"She is in my world," Grump replied solemnly.

"But how?" Tim couldn't believe his ears. "We have to get her out. Everybody here is looking for her, even the police. Her parents are crazy with worry… I was as well," Tim added quietly.

"I don't know how to get her out," said Grump apologetically.

"What do you mean you don't know? How did you get here then?" Tim was starting to lose his patience.

"I don't know!" There was a real desperation in Grump's voice and Tim understood that whatever it was that was happening here right now, it wasn't Grump's fault. He found himself here, in this weird world, as unexpectedly as Molly did in his.

"Please tell me what happened to you," said Tim, thinking the only way to get to the bottom of all this was to start at the beginning.

And so Grump told Tim everything that had happened. How he and his brother Grug were walking in the tunnels, and how a strange light had pulled him into this world. How he could hear Grug's whispers, but couldn't communicate with him, and how the same strange thing happened to Molly when he tried to scare her. He went on to say how sorry he was for trying to scare her and how he would very much like to go back home.

"It is all very strange," said Tim. "I don't know what we have to do, but maybe we should stick together. Sooner or later we'll figure something out." *Hopefully sooner*, he thought to himself; he could still see the fear and upset in his mum's face, and he couldn't begin to imagine what Molly's parents were going through.

"Where do you sleep, Grump?"

"Here in these bushes," he replied, pointing his furry hand out to an overgrown privet hedge.

"Well, you shouldn't stay here any longer by yourself; it's not safe. Come with me to my house. It's warm there and there's food, and we can figure all this out together."

Grump couldn't believe his ears. This little boy, who was begging him just a few minutes ago not to eat him, was inviting him to his home and offering shelter, help and friendship. *Humans are extremely odd creatures indeed*, he thought.

As the words left Tim's mouth, he suddenly realised he might have a problem getting Grump past his mum. "Although…" Tim continued, "I'm just not sure… well, what I'm trying to say is that, well… my mum will totally freak out when she sees you!"

"Don't worry." Grump smiled. "I still have some invisibility salve left in my pouch. Come here when school finishes; I'll be waiting. You won't be able to see me, of course, but if you stand with your back to me, I'll put my hand on your back and you can guide me home."

"INVISIBILITY! Wow, how cool is that?!"

"Did you actually hear anything else I've just said?" Grump stropped, slightly shocked by Tim's reaction to his invisibility. But then he realised that considering all the weird and wonderful information Tim had just taken on board, he'd handled it all pretty well. *In fact*, Grump thought, *this boy is OK*. Meeting him was the only good thing that had happened to him since he lost his brother.

"Yes, of course, sorry. I'll come here after school and turn around and you'll put your hand on my back so I can guide you to my car."

"Thank you, Tim."

"Not a prob—" Tim couldn't finish his sentence because at that exact moment something strange happened. The ground they were standing on shook and they could hear chanting, like the whispers Tim had heard before, from underground. They both fell to the ground and backed away slightly because the soil at their feet was starting to mount up; a weird-looking object slid out from underneath. It looked like the roots of a tree growing upside down, but it wasn't the colour of a tree's roots; it was a bright, fluorescent blue.

Tim jumped to his feet first and took a closer look.

"What on earth is that?"

"That, my little friend," said Grump, with his voice shaking and eyes full of tears, "is a message from my brother."

Chapter Seven

Mama G

Molly was enchanted with the beauty of the tunnel. She walked next to Grug, and she felt safe and happy. How couldn't she feel happy in such a beautiful place? The tunnel turned and twisted, but all the way it was lit by the beautiful, luminous, golden light. As she walked, the colours around her changed from orange to dark red, to yellow and then back to orange again – but all illuminated in gold.

"The colour change depends on the crystal or rock we were working with at the time," Grug explained, noticing Molly's fascination with the tunnel walls. "Our world is very rich in minerals."

Molly was wondering if her world was rich in minerals too, but she didn't say it out loud, because she didn't want to remind Grug about his brother's fate. She could feel how worried he already was. Thinking she couldn't see it, Grug was mumbling to himself and rubbing his brow in a troubled manner. She saw it, though, and thought that was enough worry for one hogmill. And besides, walking alongside him was very comforting. They didn't talk continually, but even in silence she could appreciate his friendly presence. It was in these silent moments that she really absorbed the wonder of the tunnel; it was really magical. Sometimes she could hear the distant noise of running water, but the path was dry and the air all around them was surprisingly warm. They had been walking for over an hour when suddenly Molly noticed the tunnel's light changing in intensity. It felt more like daylight than the illumination from the tunnel.

"We're almost there," said Grug; Molly could hear the excitement in his voice.

"Did you miss your mum?" she asked.

"I did. And I miss Grump terribly too. This is the first time that we've been separated for so long."

"I don't remember my mum. I suppose I have one, but—"

Molly couldn't finish her sentence, because suddenly the tunnel ended. And what she saw took her breath away and left her speechless. A vast, round plateau stretched out in front of her eyes. It was raised up high and she could see a path of stone steps leading up to it. All around the plateau there was a rocky wall, higher than her eyes could see, with entrances to tunnels going all the way round. In front of her another set of high, stony steps led to a tree border, visible from down below. She could see trails of smoke rising above them high into the sky… a sky that was absolutely amazing, filled with the colour of the setting sun.

"There are one hundred steps to be conquered in front of us and then there are Tree Guards we have to answer to. Beyond them, is my village," said Grug, with a huge smile on his face.

"One hundred steps?!" Molly felt like crying.

"Don't worry, we hogmills have our ways of getting home," said Grug, with a mysterious smile.

"But I'm not a hogmill," Molly said, defeated.

Grug smirked and approached the lowest step, touching the side of it with his hand. There was a blast of orange light and immediately after that, the step opened, revealing a stone bench hidden beneath. Grug gestured to Molly and she sat on one side of the bench. He took the other side and pulled the ropes right across their waists. It was very tight, and Molly was just about to protest when suddenly the bench jerked sideways and started to slide upwards with immense speed. With her hair in her face and teary eyes, Molly laughed out loud. It was pure joy to speed upwards with Grug at her side. Then, as suddenly as it started, the ride finished and the bench came to a stop. Grug undid the ropes and stood up, pulling Molly with him. They were on top of the plateau now, right in front of the ancient giant trees.

"These are the guardians of our safety," said Grug. "They look innocent and immobile, but they are very powerful. They are Tree Warriors of past ages. Every traveller has to answer to them before he is allowed to pass through the gates. You have to answer to them too, and I will not be able to do anything if they won't allow you to pass. Good luck, little human girl."

Grug took a deep breath and stepped forward. "I am Grug the hogmill. Greetings, O powerful guardians. I am coming home and bringing a guest with me to see Mama G. This is a human she-child that came through to our world. She needs Mama G's help to get back to her own world. Please let us pass, O powerful Tree Warriors."

"Welcome home, Grug." The voices came from nowhere and from all directions at the same time. It was deep and resonating, and went through the body straight to the bones. Molly shivered. She wasn't sure if there was one creature speaking or a hundred of them. "Come nearer, human she-child."

With her legs trembling, Molly stepped forward.

"What is your name?" asked the trees.

"I can't remember," answered Molly, with a small and shaky voice.

"Speak up, child," said the voices powerfully.

Molly didn't know what to say. She didn't know who or what she was, where she came from or what she wanted. She didn't know where her world was or what it looked like. She didn't know if she wanted to go back there. She quite liked it here. There was something probing in her head and she realised that the trees were inside her head, hearing every single thought that was passing through her mind, as if she were shouting them out loud. Molly got really scared. There was something predatory about those creatures, something not peaceful or tree-like at all. Suddenly there was a loud crash, and another voice spoke from within the gate.

"Let them pass! They are my guests and they are under my and your protection!"

"Mama G!" Molly could hear relief in Grug's voice.

The probing in Molly's head stopped and with a heavy sound the gates opened.

Grug rushed inside and threw himself into his mother's outstretched arms. Molly followed him in and stood patiently, waiting for the greeting to end. In the meantime, the gates closed behind them. Molly had time to take a good look at the new hogmill. Grug's mum looked similar to her son, but at the same time totally different. She was slender, and taller than her son, and her fur was purple in colour. Mama G saw Molly looking at her and she smiled.

"Blueberry dye went wrong. Too much experimenting with colours, I'm afraid. Come here, little human girl, let me have a look at you."

Molly stepped forward and straight into her arms. She wasn't expecting any cuddles, but she took this one with relief and appreciation. There was something very motherly about Mama G, and something very lovable. Even though they'd only just met, Molly trusted her as much as she trusted Grug. She was so happy she had met them both. She couldn't remember her own family, and she was glad and thankful that this family was ready to take her in and help her to find her way back home.

"Come, little ones. I was expecting you," said Mama G with a smile. "Let's eat, and then you can tell me of your ordeal."

They followed Mama G along the woodland path. Molly could still feel the eyes of the Guardian Trees on her back, but there was no hostility in their gazes, only acceptance. Molly felt they had great knowledge; she could feel their wisdom and power, and she felt really lucky that she was now under their protection. She followed the two hogmills deeper into the forest.

When they reached the village, she couldn't believe her eyes. It was the most beautiful place in the world. Wooden houses were built in all the places between the mighty roots of the ancient trees. More of them were built on the tree trunks and looked more like wood fungi, not handmade creations. There were wooden ladders and bridges joining them together. The houses were painted in bright but natural-looking colours. They all looked rather small, and it took Molly a while to understand that the living quarters were actually inside the trees as well. All made out of wood, everything round, softly coloured and beautifully decorated.

Mama G's house stood in the middle of the village. It looked a little like a small farmhouse, beautifully decorated and sculpted out of wood. Colourful plants and flowers filled all the paths around the house, and it looked like the house itself was floating in a never-ending sea of colours. From the main doors they came straight into a large kitchen with an enormous stove centrally opposite the entrance. Molly realised that this entire floor was taken up by the kitchen. There was a window in every single wall and it made the room really light and bright. There were countless cupboards going all the way around the room. Numerous plants hung down from the ceiling, all bound with colourful ribbons. The middle of the room was taken up by a wooden table with chairs and benches put neatly around it, and in the left-hand corner next to the fireplace there was a very large and comfortable-looking armchair, covered with cushions and pillows and a little soft stool in front of it to support the feet. Near the armchair, Molly saw a beautiful wooden staircase leading to the next level of the house.

"Mama G always receives guests in the kitchen. She is a herbalist and an elder of our tribe," said Grug. "This is the biggest room in our house. Our bedrooms are on the next floor," he said, pointing above his head.

"This is a really beautiful house, Mama G," said Molly. "Thank you for inviting me in."

"You are most welcome, child. Both of you sit down, let's have something to eat and then you can tell me what happened to you."

Mama G put plates filled with food in front of everybody, and mugs with a hot liquid that smelled of fields and dew.

"This is a special herbal mixture to strengthen your bodies and spirits, because I have a feeling that you will both need it," said Mama G with a kind smile.

Molly ate everything from her plate. It was absolutely delicious – red, blue and green berries, oat cakes, and something that looked and tasted like cheese, but Molly wasn't brave enough to ask what it was; next to it lay mushrooms and tomatoes and a big piece of fresh, hot and spicy-smelling bread. The whole time she ate, Molly was watching Mama G intently because she was the most amazing creature she had ever seen. Beautiful in her purple coat, kind, and at the same time she had an immense strength emanating from her. Molly concluded that she was a creature that you wouldn't mess with and you would certainly want her to be your friend; she was somebody that you could feel really safe with and that you could fully trust. Mama G looked at Molly and smiled, and Molly was sure, although she couldn't tell how, that Mama G knew exactly what she was thinking. She didn't have to say anything out loud – Mama G just knew everything. When they had finished eating and had drunk the bizarre-tasting tea, Mama G was ready to hear their story.

Molly couldn't say much; she didn't remember anything until the moment she woke up and looked into Grug's beautiful eyes. It was Grug who did all the talking. He told Mama G about the strange disappearance of his brother, about the time he had spent in the tunnel trying to contact him, and about the strange blue lights that preceded Molly's fall.

"And then she fell down in puffs of pink mist," Grug finished.

"Wait a minute," Mama G seemed to be quite excited, "puffs of pink mist? What do you mean?"

"I don't know," said Grug, "I've never seen anything like it."

"Did the mist surround her when she was falling? Think, boy!"

"Hmm, actually it didn't. She fell and the mist rose up after she landed," said Grug thoughtfully.

"Are you sure, that is exactly what happened?"

"Yes!" Grug was adamant.

"A forgetting stone!" exclaimed Mama G. "It's hundreds of years since I saw the last one. There's no time to waste."

She grabbed Molly's hand and pulled her into the middle of the kitchen floor.

"Don't move," she spoke gently and then disappeared into a walk-in cupboard. When she emerged again she was holding a strange object in her hands. It looked a bit like a tiny vacuum cleaner with a glass jar attached to it. Mama G gently pressed the machine into Molly's hair and switched it on. It made a little buzzing noise and gently pulled on Molly's hair.

"This is an extractor," said Mama G when she noticed the uncertainty on the children's faces. "It will gather up and keep safe all the forgetting mist, and later I can use it in my potions… I ran out of my old supply years ago. And quite frankly, the longer the mist sits on you, the harder it will be to remember."

Molly and Grug looked at each other.

"She's had it on her for a very long time," said Grug with a hint of worry.

"I know, but don't worry. Nothing is lost yet. I know what we have to do now."

Molly closed her eyes and let Mama G and the mysterious extractor do their job of gathering the mist. It felt quite relaxing. The purple hogmill moved the extractor all over Molly's clothes and body; even her feet weren't spared. When Mama G had finished, the glass jar was full of beautiful pink mist. *Forgetting mist*, thought Molly. *I wonder if my world is as amazing as this one.* Mama G seemed to glow with happiness. She pressed some buttons and took the glass jar off the extractor. It was closed and tightly secured now, ready for storage.

"Forgetting stones used to be very common in our world," Mama G began her explanation. "They look like stones, but really they are a type of fungi. We used them on travellers from other worlds, after they had travelled too far and got lost. We don't like to be found, you see. But they also have many other uses. They can heal troubled hearts and minds, they help to ease the pain of losing somebody dear to you, they bring sleep and rest, but in excess they make you forget everything. You can forget who you were and who you are, and this is a very dangerous thing, because it is easy then to lose yourself forever. But don't worry, my little human girl. You were brave enough to venture so far, and you will be brave enough to face what yet awaits you. And now you need to go on a quest to find your lost memories. We cannot go with you; this is a quest for you and you only. But if you find the answers you seek, then maybe you will be able to help us to restore the broken balance. The clouds are gathering above the Underland," Mama G explained, looking up to the sky, "clouds that bring nothing good," she continued ominously. "Something has slipped out of one world and ventured into the other one. I cannot see what it is, it has hidden itself well. I can only feel the danger, and that it has something to do with you, child, and with my mischievous boys. Well, that is enough for now. You will sleep and rest, and tomorrow you will face your quest."

Mama G took them upstairs and showed them to their bedrooms. Molly felt truly exhausted after all her adventures. She washed herself quickly and dived under the immense and comfortable-looking duvet. As she lay down, contemplating her day, her last thoughts were about the quest for lost memories. She couldn't believe that a little human girl like her could have something to do with the balance of the worlds – whatever that meant. She closed her eyes and let a long-deserved sleep sweep her away.

Chapter Eight

The Quest

Molly woke up and stretched her body. She felt wonderful. She listened for a moment to a mumbled conversation coming to her ears from the lower level of the house; she smiled. She felt safe and happy in the hogmills' house. Suddenly she remembered about her quest, so she got up from her bed and approached the mirror with the little basin underneath it. There was a strange-looking root lying next to the bowl of water with a little note in beautifully calligraphic letters which read, 'For brushing teeth: chew thoroughly then spit out'. Molly put the root in her mouth and bit on it. It was a very strange sensation. The root, hard to the touch, became squashy and squidgy combined with her saliva. She chewed it thoroughly, not sure if she liked its taste or not – the combination of the minty and meaty flavours was rather strange for her taste buds. After chewing on it for a moment, she spat it out to a little bin placed underneath the basin; then she washed her face, put on her clothes and ran downstairs.

"Good morning, sleepyhead," said Grug with a big smile, "or should I say, good afternoon?"

"What are you talking about?" Molly was really surprised. "How long have I been sleeping?"

"As long as you needed to." Mama G smiled and put a steaming bowl on the table. "Come and eat your breakfast. There's nothing better than porridge before a journey."

The porridge was wonderful, and Molly finished it quicker than she thought humanly possible. Both hogmills were looking at her, Grug with apprehension on his face and Mama G with a smile.

"Are you sure she has to do it herself?" Grug asked. "Can't I help her?"

"She has to go herself," Mama G answered, "but you will help her, and I will show you exactly how to do it."

This news calmed both of the children down and they looked at each other with trusting smiles.

After breakfast, Mama G took the bowls away. She approached the stove, took the lid off a pot that was cooking there and threw in a handful of herbs. Instantly the whole room was filled with a weird smell. Molly couldn't say what the smell reminded her of, but it put her mind and body in a really relaxed state. She wasn't afraid, and she felt that she was ready now for whatever awaited her in the future.

She looked at Mama G and nodded her head. "I'm ready," she said, and the strength in her own voice surprised her.

Grug didn't feel ready at all, but he followed in Molly's footsteps when she stood up from the table and approached his mother. He hadn't noticed when it happened, but by the time they were standing in front of Mama G, they were holding hands. This little gesture gave him enough courage to face his mother and declare himself ready as well.

Mama G gave them both a big hug and brought them back to the table. She sat with them and put a steaming mug in front of Molly. "You will need strength, courage and curiosity to go on this quest. You have to embark on this journey by yourself and we can't help you—"

"What do you mean, we can't help you?!" Grug interrupted his mother. "But you said—"

"It would help if you would stop interrupting me, boy, and let me finish." Mama G looked at Grug sternly.

"Sorry," Grug said sheepishly.

"Like I've said, you have to embark on this journey by yourself and we can't help you." She looked at Grug and lifted her finger up to stop him from interrupting again. "We can promise you, though, that we will look after you while you're gone."

"I don't understand," said Molly.

"This quest is a journey of your soul, not your body. After you take these herbs, your soul will leave your body behind. And although we can't come with you and help you during your quest, we can look after you here, so your soul has a body to come back to when the quest is finished," said Mama G seriously. "And it will be up to Grug to keep you safe and comfortable here."

Grug swallowed loudly. He looked into Molly's eyes and in that instant, he felt that he really was ready. He could feel the courage running through his veins, and he knew exactly what needed to be done. He gave Molly an encouraging smile.

"I'm ready, my little friend. Don't worry; you'll be safe with me here. Just promise you will come back."

"There is one more thing," said Mama G seriously, "whatever happens to you during your quest, although you will be in the spirit world, it will mirror itself on your body."

"What do you mean, Mum?" asked Grug.

Molly felt she already knew the answer, but she looked into Mama G's eyes with expectation.

"It means that if you get hurt there, your body will be hurt here too. We will not know what happened, so we won't be sure what remedies to use to help you. We will do our best, but you have to be very careful. We may not be able to help you, dear."

"Wait a minute!" Grug surprised himself with this shout. "What do you mean, she can get hurt?" He tried to process this information in his head. Then the reality of the danger hit him straight in his heart. "It can't be… Do you mean to say that if she dies during her quest…" He couldn't finish his sentence.

"It means that if I die in the spirit world," said Molly, "I will die here too."

*

"Don't go," Grug whispered into Molly's ear as they walked up the stairs to the bedroom. "It's too dangerous."

"I have to, Grug. I need to know who I am and where I've come from. I need to know who my mum is, and there is this big inter-world balance to consider as well," she said with a smile. "And of course we have to get your brother back."

"You're right. You are so brave, little human girl. I feel ashamed of myself."

"Don't be, I'm not brave at all. Actually, I'm absolutely petrified."

They both giggled.

Mama G was waiting for them in the bedroom. She prepared pillows and duvets to make Molly comfortable. She also brought the mug, which to Molly's great surprise was still steaming hot. Molly gave them both a big hug, drank the funny-tasting liquid and lay down.

"Good luck, human child," said Mama G. "Bring us back all the answers that we seek. Come back safe and may the spirits be kind to you."

"Good luck, my dear friend," Grug's voice was tearful. "I will protect you here."

Molly wanted to say something, to reassure them that she was going to be fine, but she couldn't make her lips form any words. She felt dizzy and heavy. She felt like she was falling, and it triggered some distant memory of another fall. She looked up and saw a hogmill, but it wasn't Grug. She had never seen this one before. There was surprise on his face and then everything was shrouded with darkness and Molly couldn't see anything at all.

*

Molly sat up with a start. She looked around and got out of bed. She felt very light.

"I'm sorry, Mama G, but your potion didn't work," Molly said in a small voice. There was no answer. She turned around. The room was flooded with light; she could see Mama G sitting in a chair and Grug bending over a person lying in bed, a real worry imprinted in his posture.

"She's barely breathing," Grug was whispering, "what have we done?"

Molly felt very confused, but then suddenly Grug moved to sit in the chair standing next to the bed and Molly could see clearly the face of the person lying in bed. She gasped – the person in front of her was her. She looked down at herself and felt her hands and legs and tummy; everything felt normal and yet it wasn't. How was it possible that she was standing here, unheard and unseen by anybody, and at the same time she was lying in bed? How could she see herself lying in bed? What was going on? She closed her eyes, counted to ten and then opened them again, but nothing had changed. She could still see herself lying in the bed in front of her. *This is probably how it feels when you die*, she thought. *What am I going to do?* Then suddenly she remembered everything that Mama G had told her – she remembered about her quest. In that instant of remembrance, she felt her head getting really heavy and achy. It felt like cold waves trying to get into her mind; they were almost there, but then as suddenly as they appeared, they disappeared altogether. *I almost remembered something*, Molly thought; then she realised what she had to do. She looked at Mama G and Grug one last time and left the room.

The lightness outside blinded her for a moment. When her eyes had adjusted, she could see all the happy hogmills going about their own business. She could see everybody, but she was visible to no one; or so it seemed. She saw a shimmering line of light coming from underneath her feet and disappearing up of one of the village's trees. It was swaying gently in the breeze and it seemed to be beckoning her. She decided to follow it. Unnoticed by anybody, she started to climb the wooden steps up and around the tree. When she reached the top, she stood on a large wooden platform surrounded by thick branches and leaves. She could hear the rustle of feathers, but she could see nothing. No, not exactly nothing; when she reached the platform she could see a black shape out of the corner of her eye. It disappeared when she looked straight at it and she thought it must have been a trick of the light, but she wasn't certain. She could feel there was something there; she just couldn't see it yet. But she was new to all this questing and she knew she had much to learn before she could even begin the real quest. She closed her eyes and breathed deeply. Then she looked in the exact spot where she thought she had seen something before. She looked long and deep until her eyes were watering and shaking, but she didn't stop. Then, when she couldn't take it anymore and she thought she would blink, she thought of something.

She cleared her throat and said in a small voice, "I don't know who you are or if you wish me any harm, but I know that you are here. Please show yourself to me."

And in that moment she felt as if the fog was lifted from her eyes and she could see everything again. She could see so much more than ever before – in front of her, perched on the lowest branch, sat a huge and amazingly beautiful raven. Her black and shiny feathers were rustling in the breeze. Her deep, dark eyes were piercing Molly's, but Molly held her ground and looked straight into the bird's eyes. They stared at each other for a moment and then suddenly Molly felt filled with hope, love and strength.

She smiled. "Thank you for showing yourself to me. You're so beautiful. Who are you?"

The raven smiled back at her. "My name is too long and too screechy for your ears to withstand, child. I was the queen of my tribe, but I am no more. You can call me Alithema. The spirits have answered, and I am here to guide you and help you through your quest. Come, child, there is no time to lose."

"Thank you, Alithema. I'm so glad you have come." Molly slowly approached the raven and put her hand into her feathers. They were soft but strong. Alithema flicked up her wing and Molly found herself sitting on her back. The raven opened her huge, strong wings, and they flew together up above the hogmills' trees.

The flight was liberating. Molly found herself laughing out loud and screaming at the top of her voice. She felt truly happy. This optimistic feeling spread to Alithema and the huge raven chuckled from within, with a deep and most beautiful laugh. Molly hugged her tight. It was wonderful to have a companion on such a difficult journey.

"Do you know where we are going?" Molly asked quietly.

"I think the best place to go would be the Spirit Tree. She is the most magnificent and powerful being in all the worlds. If she cannot help you, she will know for sure where you should go."

"Where does she live?"

"In the heart of the Underland," said Alithema sadly, "a long way from here."

Molly could feel the raven's strong muscles working with every move of her wings. She could hear the wind playing with her feathers, which were softer than Molly could have imagined. She cuddled the raven's back and closed her eyes. She felt as though she was surrounded by the softest and warmest duvet. She felt safe and hopeful that soon she'd be able to meet the Spirit Tree and her ordeal would end. She would be able to remember who she was and where she belonged. Suddenly the movement of Alithema's wings became more frantic.

"What's happening?" Molly shouted against the wind. She hadn't even noticed the wind growing in strength; she had been so comfortably hidden in Alithema's feathers.

"The Darkness is fast approaching," said the raven.

"Night already?" Molly was surprised. "I didn't think we'd been flying that long."

"I didn't say night. I said Darkness. Look there."

Molly looked. From the horizon a black cloud was moving really quickly in their direction. This cloud was like nothing Molly had ever seen before. It was moving with immense speed and it was accompanied by a roaring sound which reverberated everywhere around them. The roar was slowing them down. Molly could feel Alithema struggling to stay airborne.

"Hold on tight, little girl. They will be on top of us in no time at all."

"Who are they, and what do they want?" Molly asked, although she wasn't sure if she was going to like the answer.

And then they were hit by the cloud and it felt like they had hit a wall. The wall was made of claws, beaks and black eyes filled with foreboding.

"No, my children, no!" Alithema cried in pain.

At that moment Molly lost her grip on the feathers and felt herself falling. She looked down and frantically waved her arms. The ground was very far away. Molly realised it was too far for any wingless human to survive and she started to feel really scared. Before this moment everything had happened too quickly for her to feel anything, but right now fear was spreading its tentacles throughout her body, paralysing her in her fall.

*

"Mama G, help, I don't know what's happening!" Grug's voice echoed throughout the house.

Mama G ran up the stairs. When she burst into the room, she saw her son in despair trying to hold onto the human girl. Deep and bloody cuts were appearing all over the child's body and her face was frozen in a mask of terror.

"Talk to her, Grug. She might hear you. I'll go and get the remedies. I just hope it's not too late."

"Hurry, Mama G. Please hurry!"

"Hold on, little human girl," Grug whispered in her ear. "Hold on and come back to us."

*

Molly waved her arms frantically. The ground was coming nearer and nearer. But so were huge leaves growing from the trees beneath. "Hold on and come back to us," she heard Grug's voice deep inside her head. She tried to reach the first leaf. It slipped out of her grasp and smacked her right in the face. She fell into a mass of greenness. She was stretching her arms and trying to catch everything she could hold on to. She was catching and letting go, the branches smashing her with real force, smacking her face and body. But the leaves slowed down her fall and she could breathe again. And just when she thought it would never end, she thumped onto the forest floor. She lay in the moss, breathing heavily, concentrating on every single part of her body, checking for fractures. She felt like one big bruise, but she didn't think she had broken anything. She tried to get up, but she couldn't. She decided to stay where she was until she was strong enough to get up. Then she would try to find Alithema. The thought of her new friend being hurt was unbearable. But Molly was too weak to think about it now. She closed her eyes and drifted off to sleep.

*

"What are we going to do?! What are we going to do?!" Grug was absolutely frantic with anxiety.

"Calm down." Mama G finished examining Molly's body. "There are no fractures, only bruises and cuts. We can deal with them. Here, finish applying this salve to the cuts, and I will bring the strengthening herbs."

Grug took the jar from his mum with shaking hands. He couldn't see what he was doing very well because tears were flooding out of his eyes. As gently as he could he put the strange-smelling salve onto Molly's body. It crusted nicely and stopped the bleeding completely.

"Hold her head up," said Mama G, appearing behind him. She was holding another mug of steaming herbs and very gently poured them down Molly's throat. The girl swallowed and soon afterwards a healthy colour reappeared on her sleeping body.

"That's all we can do." Mama G put her hand onto Grug's arm in a reassuring gesture. "Now we wait."

Chapter Nine

She-Wolf

Molly opened her eyes. It took her a moment to realise where she was and what had happened. She remembered the black cloud and her fall. She tried to move her body, and was shocked and relieved when the movement didn't cause any pain. She stretched her arms and legs and scratched her tummy. She was all right; a laugh escaped her tightened jaw. In wonderment she remembered Grug's voice and straight away she knew who to thank for her rescue. How lucky she had been so far, she mused. She was indebted with her life to Grug and Mama G.

Molly knew she didn't have any time to lose. She gathered herself up and looked around. She was standing underneath the great tree with huge leaves. This was the tree that had saved her life. Filled with gratefulness, Molly put her hand onto the tree trunk and said thank you. She put all her love and gratitude into those two words. When she turned from the tree, the world surrounding her was a totally different place. The clearing was filled with creatures and spirits, all going about their daily business. She stepped from underneath the tree and started down the path. Some of the spirits looked at her and smiled, some waved their hands, and others didn't notice her at all. She felt that she belonged in this wonderful place; she felt at peace and very happy. She wanted to stay with the spirits, build a little house underneath the tree that saved her and live a happy life in this glorious neighbourhood. But she knew she couldn't; she had a quest to follow and a new friend to save. The path she was walking along led deep into the forest. She smiled at all the creatures in the clearing as she went cautiously along the path. The forest was dark but not gloomy. She could clearly see the path winding around the trees and disappearing into the depths within. Molly didn't know what awaited her, but she knew she had to find the courage to persist, that she had to carry on with this strange quest and try to find all the answers, not only for herself, but also for her friends. And what was more, she had to find her true self, lost somewhere between the human world and here.

Molly had been walking for what seemed to her like a very long time, when suddenly she heard a noise coming from between the brambles. She wasn't sure if she should leave the path and venture into the unknown or forget about the noise and carry on. In the end, curiosity won out, and Molly stepped off the path.

The brambles were much thicker than she'd expected, so it took her some time to go around and through them.

Curiosity killed the cat, thought Molly, slightly flustered. The noise was growing in strength and Molly suddenly realised it was a song – albeit a very strange song, which moved something deep inside her. She felt very unsettled by it and she longed to see who this mesmerising voice belonged to. She pushed through the last part of the brambles and stood speechless. In front of her there stood an old woman. She was tiny and cautious in her movement, slightly plump and quite hairy. She was bending forward, picking something up from the forest floor. She was making a lot of noises similar to those you would expect to come from a wild animal, not an elderly lady, and she was humming her mesmerising tune in between.

Without looking at Molly, the old woman spoke, "Are you just going to stand there and stare or are you going to come and help me?"

Her voice didn't sound human either – it was something between the howl of a wolf and… Molly couldn't quite put her finger on it, but it sounded like rain.

Molly felt really embarrassed by being caught out staring like that. "I'm so very sorry," she said. "Of course I'll come and help you. What are you doing?" she asked, approaching tentatively.

"Curious thing, aren't you?" the old woman replied.

"I'm sorry, that was quite rude of me. How can I help you?"

"My back is old and tired, and I haven't found what I'm looking for yet. It is here, but my eyes are not so good anymore. Will you find it for me?" the woman said.

"Of course," said Molly, bending forward and looking into the dirt. "What are we looking for?"

"We are looking for a special stone. Show me everything that you find, and I will tell you if it is the right thing," the woman replied, then she sat down with a thump on an old tree trunk.

Molly combed her fingers through the forest floor and started to work her way around the clearing. Whenever she found something, she approached the old woman and showed her the find.

"What are you doing here all alone?" the woman asked after some time.

"I wasn't alone. I was with my friend, Alithema, but we were separated. I'm trying to find her now. I fell off her back and found myself in this forest. We were looking for the Spirit Tree."

"And why would somebody so young be looking for the Spirit Tree?"

"I need to remember who I am and where I came from. You see, I'm not from this world. But I can't remember anything. When I came here, I landed on the forgetting stone."

"I see," the woman replied with a smile. "And why would you like to remember who you are? Why not just start all over? Don't you like it here?"

"I have to say, it is very tempting," Molly laughed. "I really love Grug and Mama G, I also love Alithema, but I am not from here. I used to be somebody, somebody's friend, somebody's daughter, and now I feel a very important part of me is lost. Maybe even the most important part. I would like to find out who I am and where my roots are. Without it I'm like the piece of wood you are sitting on. And besides, when I look at Mama G, I think that somewhere there must be a woman who is waiting for me and missing me terribly. I have to find my way back to her."

"Then you are double lost, *Girl Without a Name*."

"I suppose I'm even triple lost, as I have no idea what we're looking for," laughed Molly.

The old woman smiled. "Don't worry, my sweet girl. Show me what is in your hand."

Molly stretched out her arm and opened her palm. Inside there was a tiny piece of bone.

"You found my stone." The woman laughed. "Now help me to lay them all out."

She untied a beautifully embroidered pouch from her belt. It was full of bones, of different shapes and sizes. They were all very old.

"I've been looking for that little piece for many years. Thank you for your help."

Molly helped to lay all the bones out. First the skull, next the vertebrae and the ribs, then the long and strong bones of the legs, and the small ones of the tail. Although all the bones were time-worn, Molly could see they belonged to a beautiful and mighty creature.

"Now you sit here quietly, *Girl Without a Name*. And let me do what I came here for."

The woman left Molly sitting on the tree trunk and stood over the bones. She caressed the beautiful white sculpture arranged before her, smiled with tenderness and started to sing. Her song was beautiful and it touched Molly's heart on the deepest of levels. It was commanding and potent, compelling life to sing its song yet again within the empty frame. And the bones shook with the tone of the song and were filled with life. And the rib bones and leg bones began to flesh out and the beast became furred. The woman sang louder, and more of the creature came into being, with its pointy ears and strong tail. And the woman's song began to rise to a crescendo, and as it did so the wolf started to breathe. She sang so deeply that the earth shook, and as she sang the wolf opened her eyes and sat up.

Molly stood absolutely mesmerised by the creature. The woman smiled but she didn't cease singing. She approached the she-wolf and put a hand on her head. She sang some more and suddenly the old woman wasn't old anymore. In front of Molly's eyes, the woman and the wolf became one. As the wolf sat there, looking at Molly, she could see that it was really the woman's eyes looking back at her, and it was the woman's voice coming out of the wolf's mouth when she spoke.

"Thank you, *Girl Without a Name*. Thank you once more. You've done me a great service, so I will help you in return. I can only help you find your way once. What would you like it to be? Shall I take you to the Spirit Tree or to your lost friend?"

The enormity of the situation hit Molly. She knew that she should go and find the Spirit Tree. That was the reason behind her quest; only there she could find all the answers she was seeking. And yet, she couldn't leave Alithema in the unknown. She had to find her and make sure she wasn't in any danger.

"Take me to Alithema, please," the words came out of Molly's mouth quicker than she thought possible. "Please don't think me rude, but who are you?"

"As you wish." The she-wolf smiled. "I am Laloba, and the Spirit Tree is my sister. We are the spirits of life and death, of all that is known and all that is forgotten and forbidden. We are the Weaver Mistresses. There used to be three of us," she added with a smattering of sadness in her voice.

"Who was the third one?"

"That I cannot reveal to you just yet. Before we go there is something I would like to give you."

The wolf lowered her head and something fell out of her mouth. She moved it with her paw towards Molly. "Take it, my lovely *Girl Without a Name*. Take it and look after it."

Molly picked up the little object and held it in her palm. It was a tiny bone, just like the one she found for Laloba.

"Thank you so very much," she said and put the bone in her pocket. Just as she did so, she felt the bone melting against her skin and into her bones. At the same time, she felt a strong pain on her forearm; she lifted her sleeve and saw there a golden mark in the shape of the wolf claw.

Laloba laughed, and her laugh was deep and rejuvenating. Molly felt healed and whole. She knew that she was almost there, almost at the gate of her memory; almost, but not quite yet.

"Sit on me," Laloba said, "and let us go to find your friend."

Molly did as she was told. The wolf lowered herself down so she could climb up onto her back. She was a magnificent creature, fast and strong on her feet. With each mighty step, a great distance was covered, and Molly almost felt like she was flying. She gripped tightly to Laloba's fur; and with her face pushed firmly into the depths of Laloba's warmth, she could smell the new life just created, pulsating underneath her body. She was very surprised that she could feel those things and understand them. They were very new feelings to her and she wondered if they had anything to do with the golden claw mark on her forearm. She couldn't ponder those thoughts much longer, though, because the wolf came to an abrupt halt and Molly found herself in the darkness of the forest.

"This is as far as I can go, my little friend," Laloba said. "I have a feeling that you will find your friend when you follow the stony path in front of us. Have courage, little *Girl Without a Name*, and may we meet again."

With that Laloba smiled, turned around and was gone. Molly suddenly felt so small and so very scared, alone in the darkness. It wasn't friendly, and its thick tentacles reached for Molly, pulling her in further. She stumbled backwards, feeling even smaller and more scared. She saw things in the forest, scary things and tempting things; she could hear voices coming from every single direction. She was all alone and yet she wasn't. She knew that if she didn't start moving she would go mad with fear, so she ran. Forward, straight on the stony path, trying to numb the voices and blind the eyes, trying to get through to the thickest part of the darkness in front of her. When she reached that place, everything stopped. She welcomed the silence, but the blackness all around her was overpowering. She needed to find her inner strength; she needed it very badly. When her eyes slowly accustomed to the lightlessness, she saw a shape lying on the forest floor.

"Hello," she whispered, feeling her legs giving way underneath her.

She went down and felt some softness underneath her fingers. She picked it up and brought it nearer her face. Feathers, black feathers, moistened with blood.

"No!" cried Molly, and crying, she ran towards the motionless body of her friend. "No, no, no! What's happened?"

She covered the body of her friend with her own, sobbing and shouting. Her despair was great, and she could feel it resonating to the core of her being. The darkness began to creep nearer and nearer, absorbing everything in its path. Molly felt hopeless; lost. She could feel the approaching darkness and there was nothing she could do about it.

It started as a little feeling of warmth in her forearm. It increased in strength until it almost burnt her arm from within. Molly saw the golden light expand from the wolf claw mark, all over her body. She was radiating with it, the warmth brought love, hope and knowing.

"Be strong, *Girl Without a Name*," Molly heard Laloba's voice in her head. "We are connected now. You already know what to do, but I will walk you through it anyway. Be brave and fight the Darkness."

*

"Mum, something's happening again!"

When Mama G burst through the door, Grug was standing in the middle of the room with his mouth open and fear visible on his face. There was a blinding golden light shining from Molly's bed, and all they could see were shadows intertwined in a floating dance of change – the girl's body changing into a large raven and then back into a human again. The silence was broken by a strange song coming from the light.

"Be still, my boy, and don't touch anything. There is a great and ancient magic happening here."

*

Molly was singing. She felt strong; she understood, she knew. She could feel the presence of Laloba and the power of the song taking over. As she sang, the darkness started to melt away. She could see clearly Alithema's motionless and lifeless body now – every single feather, every single wound and every single broken bone. She could feel amazing power in her song, a power that was potent and commanding, compelling the life to come back and fill her friend with her song once again. And as she sang, the broken bones became whole, and the wounds healed. And as she sang some more, Alithema started to breathe. She sang so deeply that the earth shook, just as it did when Laloba sang; and as her voice soared into the air around her, the raven opened her eyes and sat up. The song and the light slowly left Molly's body, and the child and the beast looked into each other's eyes.

"Alithema!" cried Molly, and she flung herself at her friend, sobbing and laughing at the same time. She buried her face in Alithema's feathers and held on to her tightly.

Alithema looked around, memories and comprehension filling her eyes. "My dearest of friends, thank you. You saved me; how can I ever repay you this debt?"

"Just don't let yourself be hurt again," said Molly through her tears, and they both started to giggle. It was a laugh of relief; they were both alive and they had found each other, and now together they felt stronger in facing whatever challenges were to come.

"Tell me please, Alithema, what happened? I'm not really sure what it was. We hit a black cloud and then I fell. What happened to you? And why did it feel like this cloud was built out of claws and beaks, did I imagine that?"

"You didn't imagine anything, my little friend. They were my children flying in the cloud. They didn't recognise me at all. They didn't know who I was and what they were doing. They attacked with all their might, without consideration. I couldn't protect myself because I didn't want to hurt them. At the end of the day, they are still my children."

"Why would they want to attack anybody? I don't understand."

"Nor do I, my little friend. One day my children disappeared. I couldn't find them anywhere; I didn't know what had happened or what to do. I decided to go and seek help, and that is when I felt a strange pull. I followed it and found you. So I embarked on your journey hoping to find some answers to my questions as well... hoping to save my children. I have to tell you this horrible truth. Although they are still my children's bodies, their souls are gone. I could feel an overpowering emptiness when they descended upon me."

"Like uncontrollable darkness? Full of dread and death and sadness?"

"Yes, but how do you know?"

"Because this was what I felt when I found you. I almost surrendered to it, it was so strong, so intense; demanding that I give up hope and bend under its immense force."

"How did you manage to withstand this force?"

"I wasn't alone. I had Laloba's help," and Molly told Alithema everything that had happened to her since the fall.

"It's all getting stranger and more magical by the minute. I wonder what it all means."

"I don't know, Alithema, but I have a feeling that we're going to find out what's happening here really soon. You know what, I don't know about you, but I feel really uneasy here and I don't want to stay here any longer. Do you think you have enough strength to fly?"

"I feel young and strong, like somebody has taken hundreds of years away from me. I can fly till the end of time," said Alithema with a smile.

"Let us go then. Let's find the answers we're seeking, and let's go back to Mama G and Grug. I really miss them now, and I'm sure you're going to love them."

"Climb on, my little friend. I can feel the wind and the sky calling. Let us fly!"

Molly sat herself comfortably on Alithema's back and grabbed hold of her feathers. They were airborne in no time, following the lure of their quest.

Chapter Ten

The Spirit Tree

"I feel really hungry," said Molly. "How far do you think we still have to fly?"

"I don't think it's far at all. Can't you feel it?"

Molly could. For some time, her attention had been sharply focused on the huge tree in the distance. It was such a magnificent plant – its huge branches touched the sky, its leaves shimmered in the sun with hundreds of colours: red, purple, yellow, brown, orange; all making it a real colour festival. It was the most beautiful tree Molly had ever seen.

"Is that the Spirit Tree?" Molly asked.

"If it's not, I don't know which one is," laughed Alithema. "Hold on, little friend."

Molly grabbed Alithema's feathers even tighter, and they zoomed through the sky in the direction of the tree.

The forest underneath them was vast and welcoming. Molly looked at the different shapes and sizes of the trees, all amazing shades of green. She saw a beautiful stream shimmering in between the branches. They followed the sparkling line towards the tree; she looked down at the water caressing the stones and the tiny fish jumping up above the surface of the water. Everything was so peaceful. Delicate breezes stroked Molly's face and delicate warmth enveloped her body. They could hear the song of the forest, like hundreds of bells chiming in the branches. It was all truly enchanting.

Alithema landed on a patch of grass directly in front of the giant tree. They both felt dwarfed by it. Molly could see life pulsating underneath the bark; she could feel the roots of the tree reaching deep into the core of this land, into the core of all the lands there are. This tree was standing not only in this world, but it was rooted in every single world, every single universe, every single dimension, known and unknown. This was truly the Spirit Tree– the tree of all the spirits in the world, the most important being ever. Molly felt overwhelmed with everything she experienced being so near to this tree. She felt the pain of the trees being cut down in the world, and the happiness of new plants feeling the warmth of the sun for the first time. She could feel the panic of animals being chased and killed, and at the same time the joy of new life, the freedom of flight, the curiosity and magic of life. She looked at Alithema and knew that her friend was experiencing similar visions and feelings. She touched her hand to Alithema's wing and let the tears roll down her cheeks. Then, when she thought she couldn't take it anymore, everything stopped.

"Welcome, dear friends," said a voice.

They looked up and saw a beautiful woman sitting in the roots of the tree. Molly gasped when she saw her, because her face was a younger version of that of Laloba. *They must be related*, thought Molly.

"Come nearer, please," said the woman in a voice which resembled the rustling of the leaves, the sound of the moving grass and the roar of the wind, all in one.

They moved forward, the child and the bird, both on shaking legs and breathless with awe.

"Don't be afraid," said the woman. "I can see the mark of my sister on both of you. You are safe here."

I knew it, Molly thought, and the woman laughed.

"You're seeking answers, and here is the right place to ask questions. Welcome to the Spirit Tree. My name is Taloba and I am the guardian of the tree, the guardian of the spirits. My sister Laloba is the guardian of life and death, the giver of life and death, as I am the giver of spirits. We are separate, but we are one, always working together, always communicating—"

"There was another sister," said Molly without thinking. "Oh, I'm sorry," she added when she realised that she had interrupted Taloba's tale.

"That's quite right, my little friend. You listen and remember, and this is a precious quality in one so young. There is another sister indeed – Daloba, the guardian of darkness and light. But let's not talk about her just yet. I know why you are both here. I am going to help you to find your answers and then I will tell you what needs to be done to bring balance back into our worlds. Are you ready for this, young ones?"

Molly looked into Alithema's eyes, and the bond of friendship and connection was held in that look. They understood each other very well, and they were both ready for whatever was to come.

"We are ready," they said in unison.

Taloba reached her hand into the roots of the tree and lifted a chalice filled with a transparent liquid.

"Come and drink the sap from the Spirit Tree, little girl, and let your memories find their way back home. Let your soul be whole once again." She lifted the chalice and passed it down to Molly.

Molly took it in both hands and drank. The sap was thick and sweet-tasting. It tingled on Molly's tongue and numbed her throat. When the last drop left the chalice, Molly could feel an immense heat spreading all over her body. She felt so hot she thought she would burst into flames. She gasped for air and she could hear something cracking deep inside her body. She dropped the chalice to the ground, but she wasn't even aware of doing so. She could see hundreds of pictures, like mini-films playing in front of her eyes. People she once knew, places she once remembered. It all came back to her at once: the faces of her mum and dad, her house, her school and the face of the boy, the one with the strange name. She could see him clearly walking beside her…

"Hi, what are you doing?" she asked him.

"Err… hi," he said, truly embarrassed.

"What are you doing?" she repeated.

"Err… I was just, err… nothing!" She could see that the only thing the boy wanted to do was run away, but he didn't.

"It didn't look like nothing to me," she heard herself saying. "It looked like you were far, far away. What's your name?"

"Timber Green. I mean, Tim."

Tim, Molly thought... *Tim*.

"Hi, Timber Green I Mean Tim, I'm Molly."

"I'm Molly," said Molly aloud. Then she opened her eyes. She was sitting on the grass, supported by Alithema's wing. Her friend had a really worried expression printed on her face. But Taloba was smiling.

"Hello, you two," she said with tears running down her cheeks. "My name's Molly. I remember everything," she said, sobbing and laughing at the same time.

"Hello, Molly," said Alithema. "It's wonderful to meet you properly at last."

Molly was so happy she felt like dancing. Every inch of her body wanted to run around, screaming with joy. She felt free and whole once again.

"There will be time for enjoyment and celebration later," said Taloba. "Now that you know who you are, what are you going to do?"

Molly thought for a moment. "I would like to find my way back home. I would also like to help Grump find his way back to his family, and Alithema to find her children..." Molly paused, not sure if she should continue. "I would also like to understand what happened to your sister, Daloba, and why the balance between the worlds was distorted. Can you help us, please?" she asked meekly.

"Are you ready to venture on that path?" Taloba asked.

"I think I'm already walking it. It started the day I fell through to your world and met Grug. I don't know what happened and how it was even possible, but I'm here now, and I would like to help. I think I can help... I think I must."

"Very well, then," Taloba smiled with fondness, "sit down and listen to my story."

Molly sat perched on Alithema's shoulder, gently stroking her friend's magnificent wings.

"In the beginning we rose from chaos, on the day when worlds were created. The sea was already divided from the sky, so we danced upon the waves, Laloba and I, and we were happy. When we started to feel lonely, Laloba assembled the bony sculptures and I called the spirits forward. We were filled with creation. We danced towards the south and the Wind set in motion behind us. The Wind was creative as well and he blew over the pieces of elemental web and dust, and together we created plants.

"We were happy together, but the Wind became a little mischievous, and wheeling about, he accidently caught the Darkness. He couldn't control her; she was devouring everything he set in motion. She was like a little chick, always hungry and hard to control. We put all our strength together, the three of us, and we implanted light into the Darkness. And she was shining with an inner light and a power too great for any of us to control. She became the highest power in all the worlds, but the light within her balanced the Darkness and she didn't want to destroy anymore... she wanted to create. So, she finished the act of creation for us. Not only in this world, though; she created all the worlds there are. She loved what she created, so she decided to retire to the darkest parts of the universe and leave us in charge of her worlds.

"When she was leaving, the Wind got excited and mischievous again, and tore a piece of her off. The Darkness left, but she left behind a piece of herself, a very powerful piece. I took it in my hands and picked the brightest and kindest of spirits from my pouch and wove them into it. Laloba crafted a beautiful woman and I put the spirit into her. We held her hands, waiting for her to wake up, and when she did, she embraced us and we became sisters. We called her Daloba, because she came from the Darkness and from us. The Wind grew jealous that he hadn't taken any part in her creation and decided to leave us.

"The three of us were happy and we created our home in this world, looking after all the other worlds there are. We had our own responsibilities: I was the guardian of the tree, the guardian of the spirits, Laloba was the guardian of life and death, and Daloba was the guardian of darkness and light.

"Millennia went by and we were content, we were together; we created, we built, we kept the worlds in perfect balance. But the Wind didn't like it. He was still jealous of that one act of creation he was not a part of. He befriended Daloba in secrecy and started to poison her soul. And the Darkness fought the bright spirit within our sister and began to win. We watched it in horror, but there was nothing we could do to stop it. Once the poison blossomed in her heart, she rejected us and left with the Wind. The Wind knew that although we had to let her go, we would follow shortly after. He didn't want us to win her trust back, so he broke Laloba's pouch and stole one of her bones. He blew it into the forest, because he knew that without it Laloba wouldn't be able to travel between the worlds. He took our sister and left us here in despair. We didn't know where they had gone or how we could reach her, so we concentrated on trying to find the missing piece. Laloba went into the forest and I stayed here, listening and reaching out to our sister through the spirits.

"You know the rest, Molly, because it was you who helped Laloba to find the missing piece. My sister is flying through the worlds, looking for Daloba, and you are here, my friends, listening to my story. Daloba is the reason why the balance between the worlds is broken. We have to find her and stop her, before the Darkness inside her becomes the only power driving her actions. If that happens, all the worlds will be in grave danger."

Molly and Alithema looked into each other's eyes.

"What can we do?" Molly asked.

"Daloba's heart is aching. She feels betrayed and lonely with only the Wind as her companion. She's decided to leave our world behind and start a new life in the human world. But the Wind is still poisoning her; he wants her destruction. Laloba is looking for her, but we only know the place where they were hiding in this world. That's where I would like you to go first, to see if you can figure out what their plans are and where they may be."

"That's where we'll go then," said Molly. "But first I think we should go back to Grug and Mama G, and let them know what's going on."

"That's a very good idea, Molly," Alithema said with a smile. "Can I join you in your quest?"

"Of course you can, Alithema. I can't imagine doing it without you."

"Before you go, there is something I would like to give you, Molly," said Taloba, reaching into the roots of the tree again. She took out a little bottle filled with the tree's sap.

"Take it, Molly. This is the sap of the holiest of trees. It has truly magical properties. Take it and make good use of it."

"Thank you so much," said Molly, taking the bottle from Taloba. It was made of beautifully carved crystal, light as a feather. She put it in her pocket. Just as she did so, she felt the bottle melting against her skin and into her veins. At the same time, she felt a strong pain on her forearm; she lifted her sleeve and saw there a golden mark in the shape of a leaf just under the mark of the wolf claw.

"Thank you," said Molly, climbing on Alithema's wing. "Will I ever see you again?"

"Now that you have been marked by both of us, we'll be able to hear you and talk to you when you call us. We will come to you when you need us, and you have our friendship and gratitude forever."

With that, Taloba waved her hand, and Molly felt like she was falling.

*

Grug was sitting cross-legged next to the bed, holding Molly's hand. Only minutes had passed from the last shiny appearance on Molly's arm, and Grug was feeling exhausted with fear for his little friend. Mama G was sitting in the armchair, sewing something; now and then she looked up at Grug and the mysterious girl sleeping on the bed. Suddenly, something dark covered the sky and she could hear the shouts of the hogmills down in the village. She dropped her sewing and ran to the little balcony with Grug at her heels.

"What's going on, Mum?" Grug was slightly breathless with fright.

"I don't know, but I'm sure it's nothing our guardians can't deal with."

They both reached the balcony at the same time. Perched on the branch next to it was a huge, black raven. Mama G and Grug took a step back.

"Who's that?" Grug asked. "And why did the guardians let it through?"

"Her name is Alithema," said a voice from inside the room.

Both Mama G and Grug span round.

"I'm Molly, and I finally know who I am," said Molly with a beaming smile that filled her face. "Oh, it's so good to be back."

Chapter Eleven

Pips Without Cherries

Molly woke up and stretched her arms and legs. Daylight was shining through the blinds and she could hear the rustling of feathers caressed by the light breeze. She could remember yesterday so clearly – the moment her memories returned and the moment of the reunion with Grug and Mama G. Everybody had been delighted by her safe return. Mama G had organised a welcome home party and invited all the hogmills from the village. There was dancing and music and delicious food and, of course, time for telling stories. Molly told them all about meeting Alithema and their quest to find the Spirit Tree. She told them about Laloba and Taloba and recalled Taloba's tale. Everybody listened with interest and commented on their courage and perseverance. Both Molly and Alithema were officially accepted as an honorary part of the tribe, and the Tree Guardians bowed their branches in front of them. Molly smiled as she recollected yesterday's memories. How far removed they were from her previous life in the human world. Life that seemed boring in comparison, but one she nevertheless missed so much. She jumped out of bed.

"Good morning, Alithema," she said, looking at the window. Molly opened the blinds and smiled at the huge raven perched on the branch outside.

"Good morning, Molly. Did you sleep well?"

"The best ever," said Molly with a smile. "It's nice to be back in my own body again."

Molly ran to the little bathroom, had a quick shower and put on the clean clothes left for her the day before by Mama G. She combed her hair and plaited it tight. When she was ready, she faced the raven.

"There's something I don't understand, Alithema."

"What's that, my sweet little girl?"

"When I met you, we were both in the spirit world. My body stayed here and was looked after by Grug and Mama G. When I came back, it was to this body. You came back as well, which I am so grateful for, but where did your body come from?"

"I was wondering that myself," said Alithema. "The last thing I remember was Taloba waving her arm and you falling. I tried to catch you, but then I fell as well. When I opened my eyes, I was lying under the tree and I had my body back. I was alone and I needed to find you, but before I even had time to panic, I felt this amazing urge to fly. So I flew and I let my body guide me and before I knew it I was at the gate to the hogmill village, and the

Tree Guardians not only let me through, but also showed me in which house I would find you. I flew to the branch just at the moment you awoke. You know the rest."

"I think Laloba and Taloba gave you your body back so we can work together in restoring balance. We will find your children, Alithema, we will get them back."

"I hope so, Molly. I truly hope so."

"Let's go down and have something to eat. I'm starving."

"How can somebody so little eat so much?" Alithema said with laughter, flying down towards the kitchen window.

Molly took the steps two at a time, lured by wonderful smells coming up from the kitchen. When she walked in, Mama G was busy cooking something on the stove and Grug was devouring something that looked very much like doughnuts.

"Mushroom puffs," he said with his mouth full. "My favourite, I've saved you some."

Molly sat on the chair and took one of the mushroom puffs in her hand. They were soft and squidgy. She took a little bite and closed her eyes. The taste was divine. She opened her eyes and joined Grug in the act of devouring them. Mama G came to the table with the new batch of steaming mushroom puffs and a dish she had made especially for Alithema. They all ate in silence. When they had finished and all the dishes were clean, everybody went out to the garden to plan the journey ahead.

"Taloba told you where Daloba and the Wind were last in this world," Mama G said seriously. "We should all go and check this place. Maybe after seeing what they have left behind we will be able to figure out where they are now and what their plans are."

"That's a brilliant idea, Mum," said Grug excitedly. "But how are we going to get there? I don't think Alithema can carry us all."

"No, I can't, I'm afraid," Alithema said sadly. "I can take Molly, but you would have to make your own way there."

"Don't worry about us," Mama G said with a mysterious smile. "Get ready for the journey and we'll meet here at noon."

At noon they all met in the garden. Molly had a water bottle strapped to her belt, and Grug was holding quite a large rucksack and stood next to a large pouch lying on the floor.

"Where's Mama G?" Molly asked, surprised not to see her.

"I'm not sure," said Grug. "She was cooking this potion last night, and now she's put it in two bottles and disappeared into the trees."

"We'd better wait for her here…" Molly stopped suddenly. There was a strange growling coming down from the trees. The three friends stood together, looking up in fear. There was a quick movement and something jumped from one tree to another. Similar growling and jumping noises came from the trees on the other side of the friends. It all happened so very fast. A couple more growls and jumps, and the friends stood face to face with two strange creatures. They looked scary enough, and the only thing that stopped them all from running away and screaming was Mama G, sitting on one of the creatures and smiling with delight.

"There's no need to be scared, my dears," she said. "⌐re our friends and companions, two lovely tree dragons: Nem and Rod. They are brother and sister, and I've just woken them up. Come and say hello."

Molly looked in amazement at the dragons. They had beautiful but scary faces that looked like they were carved out of tree trunks, with sharp teeth like blades, and slim but strong muscular bodies. When they were motionless you could easily mistake them for logs, but when they moved they did it with grace and speed. Their eyes were red and fiery with a fierce gaze, but there was no evil or malice in them, only wisdom and the will to help. Nem was smaller and slimmer than her brother and she was the dragon Mama G had chosen as her companion. Rod approached Grug and nuzzled his head to the hogmill's chest. He was surprisingly soft and warm to touch, and he purred like a cat when Grug and Molly stroked him behind his ear.

"They are very young," said Mama G, "but strong and fast. They got quite bored with their fossilised parents and they were dying for an adventure, so I promised them one."

"But how did you know about them?" Grug asked, surprised.

"Oh, Grug. Why do you think I am the elder of our tribe? I know things you couldn't possibly imagine. The tree dragons have been protecting our borders with the Tree Guardians for centuries. Not much protection was needed, so most of them have petrified in a forever sleep. It took a really strong potion to make their father open one eye and allow the youngsters to join us on our journey. It took another potion to help their mother to move her claw and release them. Now they are free and hungry for adventure."

Her words were met with happy and excited growling from the dragons.

"Everybody ready?" asked Mama G.

Molly didn't need to be asked twice. She mounted Alithema and looked down at Grug, his rucksack on his back, mounting Rod nervously. Mama G secured her pouch to Nem's back and sat behind them.

"I know which way to go, just the way I knew how to find you, Molly," said Alithema, spreading her wings. "Follow me and try not to fall behind or get lost."

"Oh, we won't!" hissed the dragons in unison.

Alithema took off and Molly saw the dragons launching themselves at the trees. They didn't have wings, but they didn't need them; they flew from tree to tree with speed and agility. They were so fast. Alithema moved her wings with strength and speed, but the dragons were never far behind. Molly could hear Grug shouting joyfully and Mama G laughing. She felt so happy. She had all her friends with her and together they were going to save the world. Well, many worlds, actually.

After a couple of hours, Alithema slowed down and started to look carefully around.

"There," she said, looking in the direction of an opening in the rocks.

The dragons noticed the opening too and rushed in its direction. By the time Alithema had found enough space to land, Mama G and Grug were already looking into the opening. Molly joined them, with Alithema and the dragons right behind her.

"I'm sure it's the right place," said Alithema.

"Oh, yes it is," Mama G answered. "I can feel something malicious down there, but I can't feel any presence, so I think it will be safe for us to go down there to investigate."

The opening in the rocks was very narrow, so they had to go in separately, one after the other. Mama G went first, then Molly, with Grug right behind her. Nem, Rod and Alithema had to stay outside; they were too big to squeeze through.

"Be careful where you put your feet," said Mama G. "There are stone steps leading down, so hold on to the walls."

Molly followed Mama G on the stony path, slowly descending into darkness. The air around them was thick with dust and something else that she didn't recognise. When they reached the bottom of the stairs, Mama G put her hand on the stony wall and murmured something under her breath. When she had finished, a golden light started to illuminate the wall beneath her hand and then spread in veins of light all around the room.

"Why didn't you do that on the stairs?" Grug asked, disappointed. "We wouldn't have been so scared if we could see where we were going."

"I couldn't, dear," Mama G said with a hint of a smile in her voice. "The corridor with the stairs was painted with earthy clay and I couldn't feel the rock beneath. But luckily for us, they didn't paint this room. Otherwise it would be impossible for us to see a thing in here."

Now they had a little time to look around. The room they were in was quite large and carved in the shape of an oval with only one exit. The floor was littered with black feathers and little stones. They noticed that high piles of these little stones were scattered everywhere around the room and everything smelled like rotting fruit. Molly took some of the stones in her hand. They felt familiar, but were somehow out of place here, as if they were missing some important part of themselves. She had this feeling deep inside her, yet she couldn't put her finger on it.

"What are these stones?" Grug asked, standing behind her.

"I don't know," Molly said thoughtfully. "There are mountains of them. What could they be for?"

"I don't know," said Grug. "They're round and reddish, maybe somebody was thinking of opening a necklace factory," he joked.

"Oh, Grug…" Molly felt the weight of memory pushing at the back of her mind – her mum and her, sitting together at the table. Molly was crying and her mum was comforting her. *Why was I crying?* Molly wondered. The table was covered with stones that looked like the ones from the cave. And then she remembered: she wanted to make a necklace for her mum out of the cherry pips, but they were too hard to push the needle through. "Use apple pips, sweetheart," her mum had said. "They are much softer…"

"Oh, Grug, I know what they are! They're cherry pips!"

"Cherry pips?" Grug looked at the stones in his hand in disbelief. "OK, they look like they might be that, but what happened to the cherries? Who could have worked up such an appetite?"

"Look in that corner!" Molly shouted, pointing to the darker side of the room. They approached it with caution.

"What is that thing?" asked Grug.

"I think this is what is left of our cherries, or at least some of them," said Molly, covering her mouth and nose with her hand.

"Yuck, it stinks," said Grug, covering his. "It's gross! And look at all the feathers."

"I know, I think some of Alithema's children were here. We need to tell her. Let's find Mama G and show her what we've found."

"Yes, good idea, but where is she? Mum!"

"Mama G!" Molly joined in, shouting back towards the entrance.

"Mum!"

"I'm here, Grug, stop shouting. There's another room in here," she said, stepping from behind a rug hanging on the wall.

"How did you know there was another room there?" the children asked simultaneously.

"I was wondering why the light from the walls didn't spread on this part of the room as brightly as it did on the others. When I touched the wall, it gave way underneath my hand and that's when I discovered that it was only a hanging rug. I'd just entered and started looking around when you started your shouting concert. What happened?"

"Molly thinks that the stones here are cherry pips, and we've found a yucky mess on the floor that may be what was left of some of the cherries. And all those feathers—"

"Hmm," said Mama G, examining the stones. "I think you're right. I know where some of the cherries are. Follow me," and she ducked under the rug, the children following after.

The second room was smaller. The walls were covered with rugs. There was a little bed with a table and chair next to it, all made out of wood and really pretty. The room made a very cosy impression. There was a little wooden chest on the table filled with lovely red and juicy-looking cherries – truly mouth-watering.

Grug reached out his hand, but his mum was quicker, and she popped the lid closed just before he could touch any.

"We'd better not touch anything before I can examine them properly," she said with caution.

"What's that in the corner?" Molly asked.

They turned around. In the darkest part of the room was a wooden cage. It was filled with some blankets and dirty clothes. They approached it warily. Mama G took out a little knife and cut the ropes, opening the cage door. She took a stick from the floor and started to gently peel the pile of blankets and clothes off each other. Even before the last layer of cloth was removed, they could see a woman's body lying beneath. Mama G went inside the cage and gently removed the rest of the material. The woman didn't move.

"Is she dead?" Grug asked in a whisper.

"I don't think she is," said Mama G, gently turning the woman over so they could see her face. Her long, black hair was stuck to her face with sweat, and it took her a while to peel it all back.

When Molly saw her face, her legs gave way beneath her.

"Oh my goodness," she whispered. "Mama G, this is Daloba."

*

Everything happened very quickly. Between them they managed to lift Daloba and manoeuvre her up the stairs and outside. She was so light and lifeless. Molly felt truly scared.

"What are we going to do, Mama G?" she whispered. "What are we going to do?" Molly could feel the panic rising in her body; she couldn't think straight.

"Contact the sisters… quick!" Mama G was checking all of Daloba's vital signs. "She needs their help."

Molly didn't know what to do. How was she to contact the sisters; how could it be done? Then she felt the warm presence of her friend at her back.

"Don't be scared, Molly," said Alithema. "Just contact them in the way you did when you were saving my life."

Molly lifted her sleeve and looked at the claw and leaf marks there. She touched them gently and thought, *We need your help. We have found Daloba and she needs you. Please come.*

She looked at Alithema and the huge raven smiled back at her. She looked at Mama G kneeling next to the unconscious woman, and at Grug standing next to Rod and nervously stroking his muzzle. She looked at Nem sitting nearby and watching Mama G with interest. She felt unconditional love for all of them; she felt like her heart was going to explode with the immense love that was buried there. Love for the whole world. She approached Daloba, knelt next to her and pressed her palms onto her chest. She felt all that love flowing from her heart to Daloba's. And then her heart exploded.

The force of the explosion cast Molly and Mama G away. They both sat on the grass, unsure of what had just happened. Mama G got to her feet and wanted to run back to Daloba, but instead she stood rooted to the spot. Molly looked up. There was a golden circle surrounding the place where Daloba had been lying just a moment ago. They couldn't see her anymore. There were strange noises coming from within the circle. All the friends looked at each other, and then turned their eyes back to the golden ball of light. There was a noise of thunder; the light got so bright they had to cover their faces, and then everything went quiet, as suddenly as it had begun. They all lifted their eyes and saw the three sisters standing on the grass, holding hands.

*

"How... but how..." Molly couldn't create a proper sentence. Everyone stood frozen in awe, looking at the sisters.

Taloba let go of her sister's hand and approached Molly. Both dragons bowed their heads in respect. Taloba lifted her hand and gently touched Molly's cheek. Her touch was warm and strength-giving.

"Molly, you brave creature, you have come to our rescue yet again. How can we ever repay you?"

"You came," was all Molly could say.

"Of course we did," said Taloba. "We came straight away when you said that you had found our sister and that she needed our help."

"I told you we are now connected," said Laloba gently.

"Thank you," said Daloba with the most beautiful smile.

"It's getting dark," Mama G interrupted. "Let us prepare the camp for tonight and get some food cooking, and then you can tell us everything. There's no point doing it on an empty stomach." She grinned.

"You've got that right, Mum," said Grug with a loud rumble coming from his belly.

They all laughed and busied themselves with the preparations.

Within no time at all, the camp was ready and the cauldron was boiling a nice-smelling stew.

They all sat in a circle in silence, looking at Daloba, with empty bowls at their feet, the memory of the stew still alive on their tongues. There was nothing to do but for her to start her story.

Daloba looked her sisters in the eyes and started. "I'm sorry," she said as tears welled up in her eyes. "I'm so very sorry."

Taloba gently touched her sister's hand and Laloba put her hand on top of her knee in a reassuring gesture. Molly felt very touched by the scene. She looked around the campfire. Mama G and Alithema had tears in their eyes too, and Grug pretended to pick something out of his shoe. Only Nem and Rod remained unfazed by it all.

"I shouldn't have trusted him," Daloba took up from where she stopped.

"My dear sister," said Taloba. "Why don't you start from the beginning?"

"In the beginning, I was so happy with you both. Why not start from my betrayal?" said Daloba bitterly.

Everybody remained silent, with their heads down, except the sisters, who looked into each other's eyes.

"It was so exciting at the beginning when I left you. I thought we were meant to be together, Wind and I. We had fun. We travelled from world to world, saw so many amazing things. We called the universe our home, and it belonged to us, fully, or at least this is what I thought. Soon enough I began to miss you both so very much and I wanted to go back. The universe was empty without you two. But the Wind didn't even want to hear about it. He was angry, and day after day his moods got darker and darker. Then one day he brought me to this cave. He put some warding spells on it, so you couldn't find us. He said he could see my suffering and that he couldn't stand that. But because he loved me so very much, he couldn't bear to lose me. He came up with this great idea, that we would create a new being for him, so he wouldn't be lonely without me – somebody to remember me by; and that if I would leave in her one tiny piece of myself, he would let me go back home.

"I was so happy. I remembered everything you had taught me about creating and I put it all into action. We were happy again, the Wind and I. I saw him smile again; I heard him laugh. Together we created a beautiful woman. She looked so much like me. The Wind said that now was the time to share with her a tiny bit of my essence, and then, when she came to life, I would be able to go home. I thought it would be nice for him to have a companion, so I showed him my essence and I trusted he would take just a little bit of it. He didn't. He grabbed most of it in his palms and left me in the cage to see the rest of his creation, before what was left of my essence would drain away into oblivion, and me with it. He was cruel enough to let me watch everything. He contaminated my essence with hate and greed and then put it inside this other woman's body. She was ugly with hate, so he gave her the power of illusion. She could become anything you desired when you looked at her. Then Wind caught black ravens and bound them together by magic and put them on her head. She sucked all the beauty and strength out of them – her eyes became sparkling, her face soft and dark, and the feathers on her head became the most beautiful black hair—"

"Oh no, my children!" Alithema cried in distress.

"They are still alive, Alithema," said Daloba. "They're enslaved but still alive. We can get them back. We can free them all."

Alithema burst into tears and Molly ran to hug her.

"We will get them back, Alithema," she said. "You'll see, we'll get them back."

"She is evil and much too powerful for the Wind to control," Daloba continued. "She has learnt from him everything she wanted to know. He took her and showed her other worlds. She loved what she saw and wanted it all for herself. The Wind, blinded by pride, thought he had a perfect student, but she knew how to deceive him, with her sweet voice, raven eyes and poisonous lies. He taught her how to use herbs and nature to create magical potions, he showed her portals to other worlds, and when he left her alone, she practised the magic of illusion. They managed to gather great amounts of forgetting mist. They thought I would be dead soon, so they talked and laughed in front of me. She thought that because she was made from me, and I would soon be no more, she could confide in me. She was laughing at Wind, his weakness and stupidity. She said that soon she wouldn't need him anymore. She was so much stronger than he was – she had my essence, the essence of Darkness inside herself, and it was strengthened by the gifts of greed and hate he bestowed upon her. There is nothing good in her, nothing good."

"What is she planning to do?" Mama G asked, horrified.

"I don't know what he's going to do. If I know Wind, he'll run away far enough not to get hurt when he realises that he cannot control her anymore. As for her, I know exactly what she wants to do. Out of all the worlds she saw, she liked the human world the most. She wanted it badly. She thought humans would be as easy to enslave as ravens were. She had decided to take up residence there and show herself to the world as its goddess. She calls herself the Great Illusionist."

"Are you sure of that?" Taloba asked.

"Oh, she loved sitting in front of my cage, taunting me with her plans. She really believed I wasn't going to make it out alive. She is ready to conquer the human world now. She has made hundreds of thousands of cherries filled with forgetting mist. She has little creatures to do her bidding and now she is planning to deliver the cherries to all the humans and enslave them."

"Oh, that would explain all the cherry pips lying around," said Molly. "But her plan can't work. She wouldn't be able to feed the whole planet with cherries, would she? It won't work, Mama G, will it?"

"Oh no," said Mama G, looking really worried. "I'm afraid, Molly, it will work. If she gets to politicians, kings, presidents and religious leaders, then whole nations will follow."

"In that case, we have no choice," said Molly. "We have to stop her!" She hesitated and her shoulders slumped. "…I just really don't know how," she added sadly.

"If only Grump were here," said Grug quietly. "He'd know what to do."

"That's a brilliant idea, Grug," Mama G said quickly.

"Is it?" Grug was bewildered.

"Of course it is," said Mama G, packing her bag and tidying up the pots and cauldron. Grug and Molly joined in to help. "We're going to contact Grump and find a way to restore the balance. She's already in the human world? Well, we have our people there too."

Molly felt excitement spreading through her body. "We have to write to Grump and tell him to find Timber," she said. "He could help him in the human world. Why didn't I think of that before?"

"Let's go." Mama G was in a real hurry now. "Grug, could you show us the place where you found Molly, please? I will try to send Grump a message through there."

The three sisters looked around in amazement. Within minutes the camp was packed and everybody was ready to leave.

"Between us – two human children, a family of hogmills and two tree dragons – we will find a way to beat the Great Illusionist," said Taloba. She exchanged glances with her sisters and then added, "We will go with you and help you to open the split in time and space, so that your message will be able to reach Grump. Then we'll find the right place to open the portal, so we will be able to travel between the worlds freely as well. How much time do you need, Mama G, to write your message?"

"Not too much time at all," said Mama G, reaching for her magic pouch.

Chapter Twelve

The Secret Message

Grump was in no doubt that the emerging root that had just sent him and Tim plummeting to the ground was indeed a message. Without wasting any time, he reached into his pouch and took out a little knife and a small leather envelope. He started to scrape the fluorescent powder off the root and into the little envelope. When he'd finished, the root disappeared underneath the soil.

"What does it say?" Tim was shaking with curiosity. "Can I see?"

"It will take a while to decipher this message, Tim. You'd better get back before someone comes looking for you. We'll stick to our old plan and I'll see you here after school finishes."

"You're right, but please don't read it without me," Tim pleaded.

"I wouldn't." Grump looked at him seriously.

Tim had no other choice but to go back to his lessons. The afternoon at school dragged incredibly for him. He was so worried that Grump would decipher the message without him that he couldn't think about anything else. He couldn't concentrate at all and was counting every single second till the end of his classes. Not a moment too soon, school came to an end and Tim ran to Grump's hiding place. When he got there, Grump was gone. Tim was absolutely terrified that his adventure had finished before it had even properly begun. He looked around frantically.

"I knew you weren't listening," said the bodiless voice.

"The invisibility salve…" Tim whispered with a huge grin on his face. "I was worried you'd read your message and were gone."

"I'm still here, Tim," said Grump. "Turn around, please, and let's go to your mum's car."

Tim turned around and felt the heaviness of Grump's arm on his shoulder. He led them to his mum's car. Luckily, she was so preoccupied with the radio programme she was listening to, she didn't notice that it took Tim twice as long as usual to get into the car. She didn't notice her son looking at an empty car seat, nor did she hear the quiet whispers. By the time she had parked the car properly in front of their house, Tim and the invisible Grump were already in Tim's bedroom.

*

The wind that had torn the hair out of her head eased down, but the hair still floated on, invisible and constantly changing currents. Then it got caught in a magpie's tail and sailed with her through towns and villages. The hair thought, *I remember that feeling*, and it started to let go of its hairy form. The magpie dived down and the hair fell loose again. It caught on a tree trunk, hit the pavement and was trodden on by passers-by; then the current from a passing car blew the hair down the street. The hair felt very uncomfortable. It was long, thick and very black. It looked around with its beady eye, wondering where it was. Then the hair saw a boy and a shimmering emptiness following him up the stairs. It knew that shimmer; it remembered a similar thing from its previous life. The idea of this previous life was very entertaining for the hair. It stretched out and felt something popping out from its sides. The hair looked down and saw a strange-looking claw, very inappropriate for hair. The claw moved when the hair thought about it and the movement felt right. That triggered another memory and something else popped out from its side. The hair looked down and saw a wing. Not a feather, not a hairy growth, but a full-size raven wing. *How strange*, thought the hair, and then it started to feel very peculiar. Because after the wing, more body parts followed, and then the hair didn't look like hair anymore, but like a beautiful, black raven. The memories were still that of the hair and it made the transition so much more difficult. The hair didn't know what was going on. His body was achy, and he was really hungry and thirsty. Then he remembered the shimmer and because it felt so familiar, he decided to find out what it was. *Maybe*, he thought, *the shimmer is hair-like, just the way I am*. He stretched his wings and flew up, going from window to window until he found the window he was looking for. He peered inside, being careful not to disturb anyone or anything. The shimmer had gone, and there was a boy and a strange furry creature in the room.

*

It took Grump some time to become visible again, just enough time for Tim to run downstairs to the kitchen and smuggle up to his room quite a large quantity of food. He told his mum he was going to be busy with homework and that he couldn't accompany her to the shops. When she left, both he and Grump were happy to have the house free of adults. Upstairs, Grump took out his pouch, and Tim was almost shaking with apprehension and excitement. From within his pouch, Grump took out a thick parchment, a little brush and a bottle of an oily substance. Tim watched in fascination.

"This is my traveller's secret message kit," announced Grump with a smile on his face. His hands moved with methodical precision.

"How do you know what to do?" Tim asked, intrigued.

"Mama G made us practise every day for months. Grug and I became specialists in not only sending each other secret messages but also intercepting messages sent by others. That way we always knew what was going on in the Underland, and other places. Well, at least we thought we knew it all."

"Is Mama G yours and Grug's mother?" Tim was enthralled with Grump's story.

"Yes, she is," said Grump. "She is also the elder of our tribe and a healer."

"Wow, your life sounds so great: healers, tribes, secret messages. My life is so boring in comparison: school, homework, sometimes football practice or a birthday party, but that's all."

"From where I'm standing, your life seems pretty good," said Grump. "If it was as boring as you say, you would have never met me," he added with a smile.

"That's true," said Tim. "Actually, all the exciting stuff started when I met Molly. She's my first true friend. I hope she's all right. Come on, hurry up, read the message!"

Grump laughed and got to work. He straightened the parchment on Tim's desk and, using the little brush, applied the oily substance to it. It shimmered with cascades of colour. When the parchment was ready, Grump sprinkled it with the fluorescent powder that he gathered from the root and into the little envelope. Like magic, the powder started to move on the page, bringing letters to life.

"It'll be a moment before we can decipher it," said Grump. "Could you get paper and pen ready, Tim?"

Tim didn't have to be told twice. He rushed to his rucksack and pulled out a notebook and a pencil case, passing to Grump the necessary items and taking some for himself as well.

"Good idea, little friend," Grump approved. "It's always better to be ready. Sometimes the messages are very fast and disappear very quickly; you can only read them once."

"Will I be able to read your language?" Tim asked with a slight worry in his voice.

"I don't know, little friend. I really don't know."

"Do all messages look the same?"

"Oh no, on the contrary, the messages can have different shapes and sizes. You have to really look around you – they could be hidden in a spider web, in a feather flying in the air; they can be written on water or sang in a song on the wind."

"Lucky, then, that this one was so obvious!" Tim laughed.

"I'm sure Mama G was certain this one would hit me on the head," laughed Grump. "It was too important to miss. Now get ready, it's starting."

The letters on the page became more and more legible. They formed fantastical patterns which Tim couldn't comprehend. Grump, on the other hand, understood them perfectly well and was writing on his piece of paper like crazy. Tim watched in fascination. Then suddenly the letter pattern changed, and Tim saw his name written in beautiful, neat script.

Tim, it said. *It's Molly. I'm all right. Trust Grump when you meet him. I'm here with his brother and mother. They are wonderful creatures and really good. We have to help them return balance to the universe. Our world is in danger. We will make a portal to get back to the human world. Grump will help you to find it, so we can be together and face the danger with all of us united. And Tim, please, whatever happens, DO NOT EAT ANY CHERRIES! Could you ever imagine such an adventure?*

Then the message disappeared.

Tim felt overwhelmed and excited. Molly was safe. She was in the Underland with Grug and Mama G having her own adventures, but she was safe, and that was the most important thing for Tim.

He looked at Grump and smiled. "She's safe. Molly is all right… but hold on, why shouldn't we eat any cherries?"

"If I've understood correctly, they are filled with forgetting mist," said Grump.

"Forgetting what?" Tim thought nothing would surprise him anymore, but he was wrong.

"I'd better start from the beginning of my message," said Grump. "That way we'll both be on the same page. Even if you think it's not important, ask if you don't understand something. We need to work together to find the place where the portal will open."

And Grump told Tim everything he read in his message. He told him about the sisters and the Wind, he told him about the Great Illusionist and her plan to conquer the Earth. He told him that the whole group from the Underland was travelling now to the portal and that they had better get going there soon as well, so they could all meet up and make a plan of action.

"How exciting—" Tim started, but he was cut short. "What was that?"

A strange scratching noise was coming from the window.

"Don't move," said Grump, and fast as the wind, he ran forward and opened the window. Tim couldn't believe how fast his friend could be. But his amazement at his friend's speed was short-lived and was replaced by astonishment at the shape that fell into the room when Grump yanked the window open.

"What is it?" Tim asked, looking at the black ball of feathers.

"It looks like a young raven," said Grump.

"I'm not a raven," the feathery ball replied. "I'm hair." Then the ball shook itself and straightened its legs, and a little raven stood in front of the friends.

Wonderful, thought Tim, *first time I've ever met a talking bird, and it has to be a mad one.* But instead of saying this out loud, he asked, "Do you mean that your name is Hair?"

"No, I can't remember my name, but I am definitely hair. I got torn off her head and now I need to get back."

Yes, definitely a mad bird, thought Tim, exchanging a meaningful glance with Grump.

"Why were you spying on us?" Grump asked.

"I wasn't spying on anybody. I was just… Hmmm, I was just… It is rather strange, but I really don't remember."

"Do you remember where you came from?" Tim asked, concerned.

"Yes, of course, I told you already. I was torn off her head by this strange gust of wind. Then I floated in the air and then you lot pushed me into this cage. That was very rude behaviour. Didn't your mother teach you any better? Now, I must get back before she gets angry. Do you know where her head is? Well, do you?"

"As a matter of fact, we do," said Grump. Tim looked at him, shocked, but Grump lifted his hand slightly to quieten him down. "We were just heading that way ourselves, would you care to join us?"

"That is a rather tempting offer, I must say," said Hair. "Would there be any food on the way?"

"Of course," said Grump.

"That's splendid," said Hair with a happy grin on his beak. "In that case, I will take a little snooze."

Tim couldn't believe his eyes, but seconds after saying that, the strange bird fell to his side and started snoring.

"What's wrong with him?" Tim asked quietly.

"He is bewitched. He is most certainly from the Underland. We have to take him with us. I'm sure Mama G will know how to help him. He may have some useful information, you know. Do you have a box we could put him in?"

"Yes, give me a minute and I'll find something." Tim ran downstairs and Grump started to pack his pouch up again.

*

Nobody noticed or knew where the wonderful-looking plates filled with the juiciest of cherries came from. They suddenly appeared in all the shops and on the street corners. They were free, so nobody asked any questions. People ate them by handfuls and took some home for their children. Everybody got an even share. Whenever the plates were almost empty, like magic they filled themselves up again. The entire town was drunk with cherry juice, and forgetting mist swamped everybody's mind.

Chapter Thirteen

The Portal

Tim was just finishing packing his rucksack when he heard his mum's car on the driveway.

"My mum's back," he said to Grump, putting the last items in. "I think I have everything, are you ready, Grump?"

Grump picked up the box with the raven and went to the door. "Of course I am. How are we going to sneak past your mum?"

"I'll go to the kitchen and try to take her attention away from the door, so you can get out of the house. I'll see you in the garden. Are you sure we know the place where the portal will open?"

It had taken them both some time to figure it out. From their perspective, it didn't matter where the travellers in the Underland entered the portal. What mattered was where they would come out in this world, and the best place for that was the school playground. That was a place Molly knew well, and they could access it quite easily at any time of day or night. Well, it would take some fence-climbing, but Tim thought they could manage it all right. Grump also thought that because the portal would have already opened in this place in the past, when Molly was sucked into the Underland, it would be easier to create another opening using the old paths instead of weaving new threads. He explained to Tim that creating a portal is like weaving a tapestry made of time and space. You have to join the threads carefully and purposefully on both sides and then join them together. If you don't get it right, the travellers may be trapped between the worlds and may never be able to find their way back again.

Grump was slightly worried, because although Mama G was an amazing healer and her knowledge in many areas was great, creating portals wasn't on her favourite-things-to-do list. When, as a little girl, she was practising creating portals with her grandmother, she managed to trap a chicken between the hen house and the fields, and they never saw that chicken again. Mama G had felt guilty about it ever since and promised herself never to do that again. Grump hoped the sisters were much better at it and the whole party would cross over in one piece. But first they had to get past Tim's mum. Grump wasn't so sure she would let her son go out in the evening, especially not after Molly's mysterious disappearance. But they had to try. There was no other way. They crept downstairs and Tim walked into the kitchen.

"Hi, Mum," he said.

"Hi," she answered, looking at him briefly and then turning towards the unpacked shopping.

"You bought enough food for an army," commented Tim.

"Yes, I suppose I did," she said absentmindedly. "Does your mother know you are out and about at this late hour?"

"What are you talking about, Mum? It's not that late, anyway."

"Well, you'd better be off home before she starts worrying about you."

"Mum, it's me, Tim. Are you all right?" Tim was beginning to feel really worried.

"I'm fine, but off with you, I said. Try some cherries before you go."

"How many cherries did you have, Mum?"

"A few, they are absolutely delicious. Have some and then go home, before I lose my patience and call the police."

Tim ran back to the hall. Grump was waiting for him there. He had overheard what had happened between Tim and his mum.

"She doesn't remember who I am!" he exclaimed. "How many cherries do you have to eat to forget?"

"I'm afraid a couple would be enough," said Grump with sadness. "I'm sorry, Tim."

"We can't lose any more time, Grump. We have to hurry and save the world. We have to save my mum. I don't even know where my father is. Oh, Grump, what are we going to do?"

"Try not to worry about it right now. Let's go and find the portal, then together we will figure this all out."

"You're right," Tim said, composing himself. "Let's go."

They walked to school in silence. Now and again they walked past a person looking lost and confused. Some of the children were outside their houses, playing silently on the street with no adult supervision. Cars were abandoned in the middle of the road. The silence of it all was truly unnerving. All the people they passed on their way had faces dirty with cherry juice. The Darkness was fast approaching and they could both feel it. But it wasn't the ordinary darkness that night brings every evening; it was something more alive, more sinister and dangerous. Tim felt shivers go down his spine and they both hurried their steps. It didn't feel safe anymore to be out in the open. They needed to get themselves away from the streets, in the security of the school grounds. At last they were there. They climbed the fence and pushed the box with the sleeping Hair underneath it. They found the place that Molly had disappeared into, took out some blankets and made themselves comfortable. They hoped they were in the right place. Now all they could do was wait.

*

"Mum, shall we pack some mushroom puffs into the bag for the journey?" Grug asked hopefully.

"Now, which part of travelling light didn't you understand?" Mama G asked with a little smirk.

"The part where you're not allowed any food," mumbled Grug, making Molly giggle.

"I heard that," said Mama G. "I'm sure they have food in the human world too, son. Although I'm hoping we won't need to stay there long enough to find out if we like it or not."

"Oh, you would love our food, Grug," said Molly.

"Let's hope you have plenty of it left. Don't forget that Grump's been there for the past couple of weeks." Grug was losing his grumpiness now.

"I just hope he found Tim," said Molly sadly, "and that they are both safe. Mama G, are you sure he got our message?"

"I'm sure, dear girl. Try not to worry too much. We'll know everything very soon. Well, I'm packed now. Let's go out and prepare Alithema, Nem and Rod."

Mama G picked up her pouch, and although Molly was observing her putting countless objects and little jars inside, the pouch looked small and light. Outside, the daylight was slowly fading away, bringing the freshness and crispness of evening air. Molly pulled her new travelling cloak tight around her. She really loved it. It was green and soft and truly warm. Mama G said it was woven by the silver spiders of the seventh circle, and that it was a precious thing to own. Her own cloak was purple and Grug's dark brown. Grug put another two cloaks into his sack: a blue one for Tim and a light brown one for his brother. "Better safe than sorry," was all he said about it. Molly didn't know anything about the silver spiders of whichever circle, but she had been in this world long enough to suspect that the cloaks were not only for keeping you warm.

Alithema and the dragons were waiting outside. Molly approached Alithema and stroked her feathers.

"We're going to find your children soon, I promise you that," Molly said, kissing her friend.

"I just hope we're not too late, my little friend."

"We're not," said Mama G, tying her pouch to Nem's side. "We're not too late."

"I'm ready, Mum," shouted Grug after securing his sack on Rod's back. "I'll go and get the sisters."

The sisters were sitting by the fireplace a little distance away. They were meditating deeply and it took Grug some time before they could hear him and bring themselves back.

Together they approached the rest of the group.

"We were travelling with our minds into your world, Molly. The Illusionist has started her plan already. There are many people affected, but there will be many more by the time you reach the human world. You have to hurry," said Laloba.

"We cannot travel with you now, but we will come to your aid at the moment of greatest need. All you have to do, Molly, is call us, and I promise you, we won't abandon you," Taloba added.

Then Daloba approached Molly. "My sisters each gave you their gifts, but I didn't have a chance to do so yet. I owe you a great gratitude for saving my life and reuniting me with my sisters. I'm not sure if I will ever be able to repay you for that kindness. Please take this Seed of Darkness, as my gift to you. You are strong and brave enough to withstand its destructive power, and you have enough love and hope to harvest it into goodness and light. It will become our connection, and together we will bring the Illusionist who calls herself Great back to the dust that she was created from."

Molly held the seed in her palm. It was a colder and blacker seed than any other she had ever seen. Then, suddenly, the seed moved and disappeared underneath the skin of her palm. A dark line started to grow from the point where the seed disappeared and up Molly's arm; it became a dark circle beneath the golden claw and leaf. Now Molly was blessed by all the sisters, and she was ready to face the Great Illusionist. She turned around and mounted Alithema. Mama G and Grug were already sitting on their dragons.

"We will open the portal now," said Taloba. "We will project it into this stone. Please keep it safe with you, Mama G, so you can reopen the portal from the other side and come back to this world."

Mama G took the stone and put it around her neck. They all looked at each other. They were ready. The sisters joined hands and started singing. Molly could see the threads of time and space being woven together in front of her eyes – the festival of colours ending in an azure glow. The stone on Mama G's chest started to shine with the same colour, and it pulsated with light. The pull of the portal was immense. Molly squeezed her hands onto Alithema's sides and held on to her feathers with all her might. She exchanged looks with Mama G and Grug, and nodded her head. Together they walked into the light.

*

Tim was getting really cold. They'd just finished arranging the stone circle and eaten their sandwiches, and he began to regret that he hadn't prepared any more. Evening slowly became night and Tim was thinking of asking Grump if he could start a fire. Tim had never been a scout himself, and he thought it would've really come in handy to have been one right now. He smiled to himself, looked at Grump and started the fire conversation; suddenly, there was a popping sound from underneath their feet and the ground started to shake. Grump jumped to his feet, grabbed Tim's arm and pulled him backwards.

"What's happening?" Tim asked, surprised.

"The portal is opening. We'd better stand clear of it and let the others pass through. You wouldn't like to be sucked in and find yourself in some forbidden place at the end of the world."

Tim saw the air around the place where he was just standing thicken and start to shimmer. Then suddenly a beautiful azure mist came from nowhere and grew from a little circle to one the size of a large door. Then he saw shadows within: one huge one in the middle and then two smaller ones on either side of the large one. They were walking towards them, and Grump and Tim suddenly started to get worried. They looked nothing like the human girl and two hogmills they were expecting.

"What will happen if it isn't them, if it's somebody else?" Tim asked.

"You're right," said Grump. "We'd better get ready for any possibility." Grump grabbed his pouch and took a chunky-looking knife from it. Then he positioned himself between the light and Tim.

"I can't stop wondering how large that pouch of yours is. You're constantly pulling things out of it. I lifted it once and it's not that heavy. Do you have an invisible chest underneath it? It's quite cool."

"You are truly an incredible boy, Tim. We are facing unknown danger and instead of freaking out, you are wondering how many things I have packed into my pouch."

"Well, it is one cool pouch. I wish I had one like that."

Grump almost started to laugh – almost, because at that exact moment the shadows in the portal crossed over. First, two dragons jumped out of the mist and then a huge raven followed. The azure mist flickered and then it was gone. They all found themselves in total darkness. Grump grabbed Tim's arm and pulled him backwards.

"Grump, are you here?" The familiar voice came from the direction of one of the dragons.

"Grug?!" Grump heard himself whispering.

"Mum, it's Grump," shouted Grug. "Get some light in here!"

Then everything happened very fast. Tim could hear some commotion and whispers coming from the new arrivals and then suddenly he could see the stone circle they had prepared earlier glowing with light. In this light he could see two dragons looking curiously at him, three hogmills cuddling and talking, and Molly – his Molly – sliding down from the back of the huge raven.

Chapter Fourteen

The Plan

It took some time for everybody to introduce each other, and in the melody of greetings Tim took a moment and realised that he hadn't been so happy in a long time. Molly was safe and she was back in the human world. Yet she came back changed somehow – more mature and grown up than Tim remembered. The whole group sat down together amongst the glowing stones. Grump sat next to his brother. They looked alike and yet totally different. Tim could tell they were inseparable. Mama G gave Tim his new cloak. He wrapped himself in it tightly and enjoyed its warmth and softness. Molly told her story and as she spoke Tim's eyes widened, impressed with her courage. After eating all the snacks that Tim and Grump brought from Tim's house, Grug began complaining that Mama G hadn't let him take any mushroom puffs, and

Tim regretted that he hadn't brought any more food too. The dragons came back from their night hunt and Tim decided he didn't really want to know anything about their eating habits. They all gathered in the circle of stones and enjoyed being together. They knew they had to start planning the encounter with the Great Illusionist, but it was so nice to just sit together in silence, and nobody wanted to be the first one to break it. Then Tim suddenly remembered something.

"Grump, we forgot about Hair."

"Your hair looks quite nice, Tim," said Grug, "I wouldn't worry."

"No, not my hair," said Tim. "The Hair; he is sleeping somewhere here."

"I pushed him underneath that bush when the portal started to open," said Grump. "I'll get him."

"Who is Hair?" Molly asked curiously.

"We found him looking into my window. Grump was sure he is from the Underland, so we thought we would bring him with us. He can't remember anything and we thought that maybe Mama G can help him."

Grump stood in the middle of the circle with the box in his hands. He lifted the lid and everybody looked inside.

"Rooky!" The shout coming from Alithema startled everybody.

The young raven stretched his legs, opened his eyes and stood up in the box. He looked curiously at everybody and asked, "Why is the big bird shouting? Some of us are trying to sleep!"

"Rooky, are you all right?!" Alithema was trying to nuzzle the raven with her beak. "Molly, this is my son,

Rooky. I can't believe it." Then she looked at Tim and Grump. "You rescued him. Thank you."

"Well, we didn't, really," said Tim. "He found us. We just decided to bring him with us."

"You didn't abandon him; for me, that equals rescuing. Thank you." Alithema was almost crying.

"I don't understand why this big bird is making so much fuss. You'll give yourself heart failure, my lovely, if you don't calm down," said Rooky, looking at Alithema. "And the name is Hair, so please stop with this Rooky nonsense. Anyway, it's lovely to meet you all, but I must be going now. Back to her head before she gets mad. Goodbye!" And Rooky stretched his little legs, fell onto his side and fell asleep again.

"He's been like that since we found him," explained Tim. "We're a little bit worried that he may have bumped his head quite hard."

"It's the magic," said Molly.

Mama G examined the sleeping raven. "I can't detect any residue of forgetting mist," she said.

"It's like with me. I couldn't remember who I was. But luckily nobody told me I was the hair on somebody's head. It's disgusting!" Molly was really upset. "We have to help him. Mama G, what should we do?"

"I'm afraid I can't do anything right now," said Mama G sadly.

"Maybe we should keep him safe and then take him back to the sisters," volunteered Grug.

"The sisters," whispered Molly, "you're right, Grug. I have an idea." She gently took the sleeping Rooky into her hands and sat down on the grass.

"What are you doing, Molly?" Tim was really nervous.

"Trust her, Tim," whispered Mama G.

Molly closed her eyes and cuddled Rooky next to her heart. She thought of the sisters, of the golden thread that had joined them together before and through which she communicated with them. She could feel the golden light surrounding her, and inside that golden light she could hear Taloba's voice: "You know what to do, Molly." And then Laloba's voice came: "Sing." And Molly sang. The song was coming straight from her heart and entering the heart of the little bird in her palms. And something inside the creature's heart started to melt, and it felt right and good. So Molly sang some more.

Tim couldn't believe his eyes. Molly was sat with her legs crossed, surrounded by the golden light, and the strangest of songs was coming from within her. It was beautiful, and it touched Tim's heart as well. It touched the hearts of all the creatures in the stone circle. Then Molly stopped and the light disappeared. She looked around and Tim smiled at her. In her palms sat the young raven, flicking his wings. Then he looked around and his eyes stopped at Alithema.

"Mother!" he shouted, and flew to her.

*

"Thank you," said Alithema when all the commotion had died down.

"I'm so happy for both of you," said Molly. "I told you we would get your family back, didn't I?"

"Yes, you did, my wonderful girl. Yes, you did."

Rooky perched on a little branch near Alithema's head and pressed his head against her.

"Do you remember anything from the time you were Hair?" Grug asked.

"Not very clearly, but it's slowly coming back to me with each passing moment," said Rooky. "I remember flying with my brothers and sisters to meet you, Mother, but then suddenly out of nowhere this great darkness came and enveloped us in a very strong magic. We fell to the ground and when we woke up, there she was, standing in front of the mirror, and instead of us were the strands of black hair that she wore on her head. And what's worse, we really believed we were her hair. She would send us off to do her bidding and then she would always call us back to her head, and we had to whisper to her what was going on in the world. Oh, no!" he exclaimed, and hung his head down.

"What happened?" Mama G asked gently.

"Oh, no, no..." moaned Rooky. "It was us, Mother, who attacked you. It was us, who let you die..." Rooky paused, his brain whirring inside his head. "And yet you are standing here in front of me. Is this another cruel trick of hers?"

"No, Rooky, I'm all right and very much real. Molly saved me, so don't worry." Alithema's voice was filled with love.

"I'm so sorry, Mother," he said sadly, before turning to Molly. "Thank you."

"Your mum's right, Rooky," said Molly. "Don't worry; it's all in the past now. Let us think of how to save your brothers and sisters, and how to get rid of that witch from our world, and all the rest of the worlds, for that matter."

They all sat down in the circle and pulled their cloaks tight around them.

"I'm trying to think of a plan," Tim said, screwing his face up, "I'm trying really hard, but nothing pops into my mind," he said, disappointed.

"We need to find her and then I suppose we will fight her," Molly said, very matter of fact. "We have Mama G's potions and wisdom; Nem and Rod's teeth, strength and speed; Alithema's flight, courage and strength; Grug and Grump's strength and cleverness; and also us... I'm not sure what we're going to be good for, but at least we know this town and we know this world."

"My sons are very skilled warriors, good with any weapon, and you children are both much more valuable than you give yourselves credit for," Mama G said with a smile. "I think the only thing we should do now is to rest and sleep, and we'll start early tomorrow morning. Rooky, would you be able to find her for us?"

"Yes, I can still feel the pull of her magic and the call of my brothers and sisters," he said.

"Let's sleep then," Mama G said, pulling her cloak tighter around her. They all found the most comfortable position they could, and although none of them believed it possible, they were all asleep within five minutes.

*

The air was filled with the quiet breathing of those sleeping, and the gentle rustle of the trees in the night breeze, and something else, something coming from behind the furthest lying stone.

"I need to hurry. Clever me. Slith heard everything. Now I need to go to Master," whispered the creature, slithering away from the circle of stones and the sleeping friends. "I will tell Master everything and she will know; Master will make Slith important, more important than stupid ravens, maybe she will even turn Slith into her hair." He shook with excitement. "Clever me, oh, clever me."

Slith had been coming back from the errand his master had sent him to Underland for when he came upon the travellers in the corridors. Thanks to his invisibility, he could follow them, and he found out all of their plans. He crossed over with them in the portal and was really pleased with himself that nobody had noticed, not even the sisters. Now, he decided, was a great opportunity to use the speeding stone his master gave him to use in special circumstances. He pressed the stone to his mouth and swallowed it as he couldn't remember what he was supposed to do with it. His little brain held only tiny bits of information, so he had to get to the Master really fast before he forgot most of the valuable information he had overheard. Luckily for Slith, the magic captured in the stone worked, and in no time he was speeding down the road away from the sleeping party.

*

"You are indeed a clever worm," said the Great Illusionist, stroking Slith's side. "I'm very pleased with you."

Slith was so excited he didn't even dwell on the mention of his worminess. He'd successfully delivered the message and was able to repeat everything he had heard since he joined the party in the human world. But by the time he had reached his master, everything that had happened in the Underland had gone from his memory.

"Let them come to me," she said. "Let them come. I will be ready. All the creatures except the children seem to be dangerous. I will let the children come and then I will crush them all. Come here, my little snake," she said with a hint of affection; this made Slith the happiest creature in the world. She whispered something to him and kissed his glistening head. "You know what to do, my little worm?" she said.

"Slith knows what to do, Master. Slith knows exactly what to do."

*

The next morning, everybody was ready for the journey.

"I'm not sure if I've ever got up so early," Tim said with laughter. "And there's nobody here to make me brush my teeth," he added.

"You couldn't be more wrong," said Mama G, taking something out of her pouch. "I'm not letting your teeth rot on my watch. Here, take this root and chew it thoroughly, it will clean your teeth and freshen your breath."

Tim held the funny-looking black root in his hands. "It stinks," he said. "What on earth is it?"

Mama G finished distributing roots to all of their party. "It's a root of a Tootipasti weed – excellent for cleaning teeth when camping or… on a quest."

"Don't worry, you'll get used to the taste," said Grump with laughter.

"I'm not so sure of that," said Molly. "I've been trying to get used to it for some time now, and I still detest it. You'll never complain about brushing your teeth with normal toothpaste after this, I can promise you," she said, laughing.

"Tootipasti," Tim murmured to himself, "that's ridiculous."

Within five minutes, everybody was ready to go.

"I wish we could have some breakfast," complained Grug. "I knew that bringing mushroom puffs would have been a great idea."

"Don't worry, Grug," said Molly, "I'm sure we can get some food in town."

"And how do you imagine us doing that? We can't exactly go to the shop, can we?" Grug wasn't convinced.

"I have to say, I didn't think of that," said Molly.

"It may be easier than you think," said Tim. "Town isn't the same as you remember it, Molly. Now that so many people have eaten the cherries, it's like a ghost town."

"Maybe it would be wise if we keep in the shadows of the trees, the dragons and I," said Alithema. "Just as a precaution."

"I think you're right," said Mama G. "The rest of you, pull your cloaks tightly around you and put your hoods up. Let's go, we don't have much time."

They gathered their pouches and pulled their cloaks tight around them.

"I'll try to sense my brothers and sisters," said Rooky, taking off. "Follow me!"

They climbed over the fence. The street outside the school grounds was deserted. Even though it was very early in the morning, everything around them seemed too quiet. They walked up the road undisturbed. Rooky flew overhead in the direction of the town square. Through tiny streets and back alleys, they found their way to the square. It was all so eerie for the children. The town square, usually alive with noise and movement, was now quiet and still.

"Where is everybody?" Tim couldn't believe his eyes.

Rooky was circling around the square. Alithema and the dragons joined the rest of the party next to the little fountain in the middle of the square.

"I don't like it one bit." Alithema was nervously looking around. "It doesn't seem right."

"No, it doesn't," said Mama G. "We'd better get away from here. I have a bad feeling."

Just then, they heard a whooshing noise and Rooky fell down straight into Mama G's arms. She examined him quickly.

"Don't worry, Alithema, he is unconscious, but otherwise unharmed. Molly, can you hold him for a minute, please?"

"Who could have done it—" Tim's sentence was cut off short. They looked around the square. From every door and from behind every corner, people were coming out: men with branches and rakes in their hands, women with serving spoons and ladles, and children holding strange-looking toys, their faces blank and unsmiling, as if in a trance.

Molly muffled a scream. "My parents are there," she whispered.

"I can see them," Tim whispered back. "My mum's there too. And all my neighbours and teachers—"

"Tim, look," said Molly. "All the children from school, the whole town's gathered here."

"They don't look friendly," Grump noticed.

"Because they're not," said a voice. "We were waiting for you."

The friends turned around. On the fountain, in the spot that was empty five seconds ago, sat a creature.

"What a huge worm—" started Tim.

"How dare you!" hissed the creature, and before anybody knew what was going on, he threw on Molly and Tim a sticky liquid from the little bottle he was holding in his tail. Both children disappeared instantly.

"What have you done?" Grump shouted, and made a move towards the creature.

"Take them down!" was all the creature said; and then all hell broke loose.

Chapter Fifteen

The Labrynth

"Get off me, Molly," moaned Tim, trying to push his head out of the soil.

"I'm so sorry, Tim." Molly jumped to her feet, helped Tim up and tried to clean the soil off his head. "Do you know what happened?" she asked, looking around.

"My guess would be some kind of portal." Tim was looking around too. "Although, I have no idea where we are; it doesn't look like our world."

"No, it doesn't," Molly replied. "I wonder what's behind those huge walls."

"I think I can tell you that in just a second," said the little voice from behind them.

Both children turned around, startled. There on the ground sat a little raven, cleaning soil from his feathers.

"Rooky!" they both exclaimed.

"But how?" Tim asked, surprised.

"Don't you remember? Mama G asked me to hold him just before we were thrown here. Are you all right, Rooky?"

"Yes, I'm fine, thank you. Slightly dizzy and soiled, but I've been worse. OK, I'm ready now," he said, and took off.

"Be careful," said both children at the same time.

The world they were in was dark and cold. Huge stone walls surrounded them and the soil at their feet was black and dry. The sky above the walls was dark and cloudy, like in the moments before a storm. They couldn't see any plants, or any form of life, for that matter. Everything was eerily quiet. Rooky disappeared above the walls, and both children felt quite uneasy and worried. He reappeared after five minutes.

"It's a stone labyrinth," he said, perching at the children's feet. "I've seen some commotion in the middle and I think my brothers and sisters are there, but I cannot be sure. It's dark at the bottom of the walls, so I can't see what's hiding down below, but I don't think it's anything good. It's a creepy place, I must say."

"Thank you, Rooky," said Molly. "I don't think we have any choice but to enter that labyrinth. Can you be our eyes in the sky?"

"Of course. We have to start over here. Follow me."

"I'm scared, Molly," said Tim.

"So am I," she replied. "But at least we're together here. I wouldn't like to wake up here all by myself."

"Neither would I." Tim smiled. "And we have Rooky, our eyes in the sky."

The children smiled at each other encouragingly and, holding hands, they followed the raven.

*

Grump was a skilled warrior. He was using the wooden bat that he had snatched from the first human that had tried to hit him. He was trying to make a passage to the worm. He knew that it was the worm's fault that Tim and Molly had disappeared, and he wanted to get some answers from him. The worm didn't look very brave, but he was hiding behind battling humans.

"Don't hurt any humans," Mama G said, so Grump tried very hard for his blows to be gentle enough to knock the people out, but without really hurting them. Luckily the women and children kept at a distance. They were all as if hypnotised, in a weird trance, not responding to anything but the worm's voice. Grump could see his brother pushing men away with a rake and Mama G dancing away with her beautiful skill of the hogmills' martial arts. Nem and Rod looked quite annoyed that they couldn't use their teeth, but they were shoving people away with their tails quite successfully. Alithema took off and was circling somewhere above them. Grump knew he had to get to the worm, so he pushed forward.

*

Slith was enjoying the show. He felt magnificent, important and invincible. He had the power that he had always dreamt of. He found it incredible that all this power lay in a little stone that his master had given him. Whatever he said, the humans did. *Keep them busy until I'm done with the children*, was all his master had wanted, and he planned to deliver. It was a wonderful feeling to have power over the others, just like his master. He was the master now; the master of humans.

Slith was so busy enjoying the mayhem he had created; he was so very drunk with the feeling of power, that he didn't notice a circling shadow above his head. The shadow grew bigger and bigger as the approaching bird flew nearer and nearer to Slith. Yet the worm still hadn't noticed a thing. Then, suddenly, darkness from the sky came upon him. The last thing he remembered was a huge, open beak, and then Slith was no more.

*

The worm was huge and juicy, and it took Alithema a few seconds to swallow it.

"Stop!" she shouted when she was done. To her surprise, all the people stopped at once. She looked around for her friends. They were all intact, tired and breathing heavily, but all right.

"What a brilliant move, my dear friend," said Mama G.

"Nicely done." Grump smiled with approval.

"I really didn't think about what I was doing. It was the instinct that took over me. I'm so sorry." Alithema looked really sad.

"Why are you sorry?" Grug asked. "I don't want to complain, but I was getting rather tired trying to fight the humans off without hurting them. You should be pleased with yourself."

"Yes, I'm happy we don't have to fight any more, but what about Molly and Tim? How are we going to find out where the worm sent them?"

"Fair point," noted Grug, "I didn't think of that. I just have one question to ask before we start worrying about the children. Why did the humans stop when you told them to?"

They all looked at Alithema.

"I actually have no idea," she said. "When I ate that worm I just wanted them to see that their boss was gone. I was hoping that they would stop, but I didn't know they would actually listen."

"They all look so creepy," said Grump. "They must have been magically hypnotised."

"Alithema, could we check something, please?" said Mama G pensively. "Could you tell them all to go home and go to sleep?"

"I can try," said Alithema, and she stood up tall by the fountain. "Please, humans, go home and go to sleep in your beds. I will call upon you if I need you."

To everybody's surprise, all the people turned around and left the square. Within five minutes, the friends were left alone.

"Well done," said Mama G with a smile.

"How did you know?" Grug asked, surprised.

"I figured out that whatever power the worm held over humans must have gone over to you once you ate it," Mama G explained. "Hopefully it's long-lasting and we won't have to worry about not hurting them again. Now we can concentrate on getting the children back."

"How are we going to do that?" Grug asked miserably.

*

The children had been walking for what seemed like a very long time. Rooky, circling above them, showed them the right way to go. The labyrinth was dark and spooky, and if not for their little flying friend, the children would have been lost in it forever.

"Are we far from the middle, Rooky?" Molly asked.

"Not too far," came the answer from above.

"Could we have a rest, please?" moaned Tim. "Gosh, I'm so hungry."

"I don't think we can get anything edible here," Rooky crooned. "It all looks pretty much the same: stony, cold and dark. No habitation whatsoever."

"Let's just sit down for a minute and then we can carry on walking once we've rested," said Molly.

"You sit down and rest," said Rooky, "and I'll fly and check if we can get to the middle without any trouble. Be back in a jiffy."

"Jiffy, it's such a funny word, don't you think, Tim?"

But Tim didn't answer. He was standing with his back to Molly, looking intensely at the wall.

"What is it, Tim?"

"I don't know," he answered. "It just looks so pretty."

"What looks pretty, Tim? I can't see anything."

"This light," said Tim, and he pushed his hand into the wall.

"I can't see any light, Tim," said Molly. "You'd better not touch anything."

"I thought it was a stone, but it feels like jelly."

"Tim, take your hand out of there!" Molly shouted,

grabbing Tim's other hand and trying to pull him away.

"There's a lever inside," Tim whispered.

"Don't touch it, Tim!" Molly was gathering all her strength to pull Tim away when suddenly the stony floor disappeared from underneath their feet. They found themselves hanging – Molly was holding on to Tim's hand and he was holding for dear life on to the stony lever in the wall.

"I can't hold on much longer, Molly!" Tim shouted. "We're too heavy!"

Molly looked down. She couldn't see anything, and cold darkness was swallowing her feet. Yet deep inside, she felt that this was exactly the right place for them to be.

"Molly, I can't…" Tim's voice was becoming weaker. "I can't…"

"Let go, Tim," she said.

"What?!" Tim shouted with the rest of his strength.

"Tim, it's OK, let go!"

So he did.

*

"Do you think we can scry for them?" Grump asked, looking at Mama G expectantly.

"Scry?! It's not even a word," said Grug.

"Yes, it is, you—"

"Boys!" Mama G stopped the predictable argument before it had a chance to develop. "We are all worried, and arguing won't help."

"Sorry, Mama G," they said, and both smiled at each other. "If we just knew what to do—"

"That would probably help," Alithema pushed in, "and I'm sorry for changing the subject. Not that I'm not worried about the children, but right now I would like to know WHAT IS THAT?!" And she pointed her wing towards the far side of the street joining the market square.

They all looked up. In the distance they could see a black mass of something quickly approaching the square. Mama G took a pair of binoculars out of her pouch.

"Nicely prepared," Grug complimented with a smile. "What can you see?"

Mama G's face fell. "Quickly, find yourself real weapons," she said, passing the binoculars to Grump. "This time we will fight for our lives."

"What is it, Mama G?" Grug asked, her words sending a current of fear through his body.

"Spiders!" Grump shouted, taking the binoculars away from his eyes. "Huge, black, creepy spiders!"

"They are spiders of the stone labyrinth," Mama G said in a quiet voice. "They are vicious, cruel and deadly. We have a hard battle in front of us."

All the friends scattered around to look for additional weapons to fight with. They didn't want to fight, but they knew they had no choice. Just the thought of fighting made them feel very uncomfortable. Nem and Rod sat down and licked their sharp teeth. The dragons were looking forward to using their teeth in a real battle. Suddenly, for them, the journey and the whole adventure had become even more worthwhile.

*

Molly and Tim found themselves bouncing for a few moments before everything stopped and they settled in total darkness.

"Are you all right, Molly?" Tim whispered at Molly's side.

"I'm fine. Are you?" Molly answered.

"Yes, just wait a second," he said, and everything started bouncing again.

"What's happening?" Molly asked, surprised.

"I'm just trying to get something out of my pocket," said Tim. A few moments later light flashed from his outstretched hand. "It's a bike light. I forgot I had it in my pocket until I landed on my side," he said with a smile.

"You're brilliant, Tim," said Molly, sitting up. "Where are we?"

"Do you like spiders?" Tim asked quietly.

"I'm not crazy about them, why?"

"Well, I'm afraid you won't like the answer to your 'where are we?' question then."

Molly looked around. They were sitting on a thick, dirty spider web.

"It's a huge web," she said quietly. "I don't want to imagine the creature that built it."

"You don't have to imagine it," said Tim. "It's right behind you. But don't worry, I think it's dead."

Molly slowly looked behind her. There on the dirtiest part of the web lay a huge spider. With shaking and bouncing knees, she approached the creature.

"Oh, Tim," she said. "Look at her, she's beautiful."

Tim looked. The spider was indeed the most amazing one he had ever seen. She had a slim but strong build, her legs were slender and her face was truly beautiful. When he approached her, he could see that depending on where he shone his light, her colour changed from green to blue with a trace of red. He had never seen anything like it before.

"Tim, she's hurt, but she's still alive," said Molly. "I think I can heal her."

"Well, yes," said Tim. "At least then we can be eaten by something pretty," he said sarcastically.

"I don't think she lives here, Tim. I think she fell in here just like us."

"Molly, I don't think we should touch it. I'm really not that fond of spiders and this one is huge." Tim was trying very hard to remain brave, but spiders had been his phobia for many years now. "I really don't like it here. We should get away as quickly as we can," he added.

Molly looked at him and saw true fear in his eyes. "I can help her, Tim. I know I can, and I have a feeling that I should. Can you help me to heal her?"

"Me?" Tim asked, surprised. "How can I help you? It's you who has magic inside, not me."

"You have more magic inside you than you realise, Tim," Molly answered, and took his hand. "Will you help me?"

"I will," he said after a moment of hesitation, "but I hope you know what you're doing."

Tim followed Molly along the web to the body of the spider. She was truly magnificent, and when Tim looked into her face, he discovered that he wasn't that scared anymore.

"What shall I do, Molly?"

"Put your hands here, on each side of her face," she said, and guided his hands. Tim saw huge fangs sticking out of her mouth and swallowed loudly.

"Please keep your hands here, and don't move," Molly added.

"OK," Tim replied. "Will it matter if my hands shake?"

"No, it won't matter, Tim. I think you're very brave."

Before Molly moved away from Tim, she leant in towards the spider and said in a quiet but strong voice, "My name is Molly, and this is Tim. We are your friends and we are going to help you now. Please don't hurt us when you regain your full strength."

After that, Molly stepped away and moved towards the spider's abdomen.

"Are you ready, Tim?"

"As ready as I'll ever be," he said, and smiled. He found it very strange that he could smile in this kind of situation. Ordinarily, just looking at spiders was enough to send him running, but right now he not only remained still, but was also holding a giant spider's head in his hands. *Life is full of surprises*, he thought.

Then he heard Molly singing. Just like before, the power behind her voice made him wonder. He could feel warmth emanating from the spider's body; warmth and strength. Her legs moved slightly and then her body started to shake. Tim felt it on a deep level because he still held his hands on the spider's face. He looked at her and saw a true beauty behind her scary façade. Then two things happened at once. The spider opened all of her eyes and all of them looked at Tim. He could see his face reflected in them. Eight Tims were looking back at him with a pretty shocked facial expression.

Then he heard a very powerful voice calling from above: "Let go of Lady Sabine's body gently and we will let you die quickly and painlessly."

Then, before Tim even realised what was happening, Lady Sabine was up on her feet, towering above the kneeling children and protecting their bodies with her own.

"You will not do such a thing, Thorn." Tim could hear her voice vibrating through the web and then his own body. "These human children have just saved me, and from now on you are going to protect them with your own lives."

"Yes, my lady," said Thorn gently, and then he shouted, "Everyone, step down!"

Tim looked up. Above them he could see several spiders relaxing from their war stance. They were spiders of different shapes and sizes, but all of them massive and in armour. He breathed a sigh of relief, got to his feet and then looked at Lady Sabine. She was taller than they were. Her body was strong and agile, and shimmered with beautiful colours. Standing healthy in front of them, she was even more magnificent.

"Thank you, Molly. Thank you, Tim. You saved my life," she said, looking at the children. "This is a debt that will be hard to repay; I promise to be your friend till the end of eternity. My name is Sabine and I am the queen of the spiders of the seventh circle." Both children gasped in recognition and surprise. "By the way, I really like your cloaks," she added, laughing.

*

The spiders were very near now. They could see them with their own eyes.

"If you can, strike them in the eyes," Mama G said quietly. "They'll be useless without their sight. But be very careful of their fangs. Their venom is poisonous and very painful."

"They are huge," said Grug with disgust in his voice. "Huge and hairy and they look pretty evil."

"They are evil and they are trouble. Brace yourself and fight well."

"I don't want to be a bringer of bad news, but how can we get out of this mess alive?" Alithema asked sadly. "There are six of us and hundreds of them."

"Have faith, my friend. Have faith in Molly, Tim and the sisters. It cannot be the end just yet. I have a feeling that we just have to buy them a little bit more time."

"We'll try our best, Mum," said Grump. "If this is the last thing we do, well, it was great to know all of you, and I consider you all my family now."

All of the friends looked at each other and there was understanding, love, courage and determination in their gazes. The dragons roared like never before and then the black spiders struck.

*

Using a seat made out of the web, Molly and Tim were lifted back up to the labyrinth. It was as dark and gloomy as before. When they got off the seat and stood up, something black fell from the sky and started to fly around their heads, making an unbelievable noise.

"Shall we silence the little bird, my lady?" Thorn asked.

"Please don't," Molly answered very quickly. "This is our friend Rooky."

"Very well," answered Thorn.

"Rooky, we're so happy to see you." Molly cuddled the little raven.

"I'm so happy to see both of you alive. I was so worried. You weren't here when I came back, and there was a hole and those creatures were coming down, whispering about humans, and…" Rooky looked nervously around.

"Don't let the spiders freak you out," added Tim. "They look scary, but they are friendly towards us – Lady Sabine herself promised."

"Lady Sabine," said Molly, addressing the queen. "This is our friend Rooky. He went to scout the labyrinth just before we fell into the hole. Rooky, this is Lady Sabine, queen of the spiders of the seventh circle."

"Dear children, from now on your friends are our friends as well," the queen answered. "May your wings carry you safely, Rooky."

"Your beauty and kindness turns the sky scarlet in embarrassment and awe, my queen," said Rooky with a little bow.

"You are very well brought up, my little friend," said Lady Sabine with a smile. "What are you doing here in this spirit-forgotten place? Two human children and a young raven – it's very unusual company to find in these regions."

"We'd better tell you everything from the beginning," said Molly, and she started their tale.

"I see," said the queen in a musing voice when the children had told her both sides of their story. "So this is why you are in the stone labyrinth. I'm surprised the dark spiders haven't shown up yet."

"Do you think that the dark spiders are in league with the Great Illusionist?" Molly asked, looking at the queen.

"That wouldn't surprise me. I wonder what she has promised them," Lady Sabine added.

Just then, a faint drumming sound reached their ears. All the spiders stood motionless, listening.

"I see," said Lady Sabine when the drumming stopped. "At least we know now why we haven't seen any of the dark spiders yet. Your other companions – three hogmills, two dragons and the raven – they are in trouble," she added, looking at the children.

"What do you mean?" Worry was audible in Tim's voice.

"My scouts have found the tracks left by the dark spiders. They led them to the human world. Well done, Thorn, for sending them there."

"We were looking for you, my queen. There were a great number of us in the stone labyrinth, and nobody even tried to stop us. I found it very suspicious, so I sent the scouts to look for the tracks. I'm sorry for not reporting that earlier. We were all so distracted with the children's tale," Thorn added.

"I understand." The queen smiled at her warrior.

"What are the dark spiders doing in our world?" Molly asked in a small voice.

"They're fighting your friends, and I'm sorry to say I don't think your friends will last much longer."

"Oh no, we have to do something!" Tim shouted, horrified. "They're our friends and you have to protect your friends and help them and…" He broke down in tears.

Molly hugged him very tightly. "I'm not sure there's anything we can do now, Tim," she said sadly. "Our mission is to find the Great Illusionist and to stop her; we have to push on and hope that they will be all right. We have to complete our mission; if we fail, all the worlds will end up in chaos." Molly's voice cracked as she spoke; she could no longer keep on the mask of bravery that had been so firmly fixed to her face. They were both crying now.

"Don't cry, children," said the queen in a very choked voice. "You are very brave, and you are not alone. We will help you. Send a message, Thorn, gather the troops."

"Yes, my lady." Thorn stood back on four legs and lifted the other four up. He took out a little drum and, holding it in two legs, used the other two to drum the message. The song of the drum wasn't loud, but it carried powerfully along the spider web to all the spiders of the seventh circle.

"Marys, please inform all the other circles of our plans," the queen addressed the smallest of the spiders.

"Yes, my queen." Within seconds Marys was drumming away on a different drum. Although she was standing right next to the children, they couldn't hear any sound coming from the drum, but the vibrations filled their whole bodies.

"I'm sending my troops to fight alongside your friends. Tim, will you accompany Thorn to the battle?" Lady Sabine looked at Tim expectantly.

"Yes, I will." Although Tim wanted to accompany Molly to the centre of the labyrinth, he also wanted to be next to Grump right now to check if his friend was all right.

"Molly, I'll come with you to the centre of the labyrinth and we will face the Great Illusionist together," said the queen.

"Thank you so very much," said Molly, wiping the tears away. "Please hurry; they really need our help now."

"Are you ready, Tim?" Thorn asked with a smile. "There's nothing better than the brotherhood of battle."

"I don't know," said Tim. "I've never been in a battle before."

Thorn lowered his body to the ground for Tim to climb up onto his back.

Tim looked down at Molly. "Good luck, Molly. I'll see you soon. Stay safe."

"Good luck, Tim. Stay safe."

Their eyes lingered on each other's as they spoke.

"Here, my young warrior," said the queen, holding up an object wrapped in a cloth. "May it serve you well. You are a warrior of the seventh circle now."

From inside the cloth, Tim took out a long, silver spider fang – sharp and deadly.

"Thank you, my lady. I will make you proud."

"Get the troops, Thorn, and fight well. Marys, choose six warriors to accompany us to the centre of the labyrinth."

"Yes, my queen," said Marys, calling out the names of the warriors who were to go with their queen.

"Please be careful," said Thorn, and he bowed before his queen. Then he turned around and sped away, taking the rest of the warriors with him.

"It's time for us to go, Molly," said the queen. "Please sit on my back." She lowered herself down for Molly to climb up.

"Let's finish with this Illusionist nonsense," said Molly.

Chapter Sixteen

The Great Illusionist

They were flying. The spiders were faster than the wind. They ran, swung from web to web and jumped distances that Tim thought were impossible. He was laughing out loud and shouting with pleasure. He felt free and invincible. Thorn found a little leather belt and Tim strapped his silver fang to his side. He could feel it hanging there now and was slightly worried whether that was enough to make him a real warrior. They were approaching the portal to the human world.

"They didn't even bother to close the portal behind them," said Thorn. "May, Silver and Truck, stay behind and guard the portal. Don't let anything else go through."

"Yes, my lord," said the hugest of all the spiders; Tim thought that must have been Truck. He reckoned this name suited the spider really well and he smiled at his thoughts.

"Hold on, Tim," said Thorn. "We're going through."

They whooshed through the portal and found themselves not far from the market square in Tim's town. They could see the commotion up ahead and the marauding black spiders lingering at the back of their troops.

"Shall we give them something to do, my lord?" asked one of the spiders on Tim's left.

"They look bored and in need of some exercise," laughed another.

"That will be necessary, Arrow," Thorn looked around. "Engage!" he shouted. "Don't kill if you don't have to! Take prisoners when you can! Protect Tim's friends! Do not touch the humans!"

"Yes, my lord!" The shout from a hundred voices vibrated in Tim's ears.

He started to feel the fever of battle in his veins. He felt weirdly ready. He reached down and pulled the fang out of his leather belt. "Now, Lord Thorn, let's go and find my friends," he said.

*

Grump was getting really tired. He had lost sight of his mother and brother. He could barely hear the roar of the dragons. He didn't know where Alithema was at all. He felt a strong push from behind and lost his balance. He tumbled to the ground, turning around at the last moment. He saw a dark, hairy spider towering above him. *This is the end*, thought Grump. *I don't have the strength to fight anymore.* The hand holding the wooden bat fell to his side. He was ready and strangely at peace.

Then, suddenly, something very unexpected happened. He saw a flash of green and blue light, and something silver struck the black spider and threw it motionless on its side. His place was taken by a different spider – tall, slender and friendly-looking. On his back sat Tim, holding a silver weapon in his hand. There was a look of astonishment and disbelief on the boy's face.

Tim looked down at Grump. "Just as I thought, everybody is fighting and you've decided to take a nap," he said with a huge smile on his face. "But seriously, I'm so happy we've found you. Take my hand; climb on. Lord Thorn will help us to find the rest of our party."

Grump felt a new strength filling him up. He smiled and, grabbing Tim's hand, pulled himself onto the spider's back.

"Thank you both so very much," he said. He put his hands around Tim's waist and squeezed it tightly. "I thought I would never see you again, my friend," he whispered in Tim's ear.

"I was worried about that too, but not anymore," said Tim.

They looked around. From the spider's back, Grump could see further around. Both spider clans were engaged in a ferocious battle. Alithema was flying above, throwing stones onto the black spiders' backs. She waved to them and winked her eye. She was in her element. Nem and Rod were fighting side by side with Arrow and another spider whose name Tim didn't know. They were slashing with their teeth and with their tails. They looked happy and full of energy.

"That's young dragons for you," said Thorn. "And what fine dragons they are indeed."

The dragons heard the praise and, after roaring their gratitude, got back to fighting with redoubled vigour.

"Look at me," came a voice from behind them. They turned their heads around. It was Grug, sitting on a beautiful red spider. A huge smile adorned his face. "I'm a spider rider, whoop!"

And right in front of them, Mama G was mounting a green and purple one. "It's so nice to see you again, Mama G," said the spider. "I'm sorry I couldn't get to you faster."

"Thank you so much for coming to help us," said Mama G. "It's so lovely to see you again, Topaz. Lord Thorn." She bowed her head towards the spider Tim and Grump were sitting on. "Thank you."

"We would have come to your aid regardless of young Molly's favour, Mama G. You have been a friend of our clan for years and we all bestow great affection on you."

"I gather Molly is well then," she replied.

"She is under the friendship and protection of Lady Sabine in the stone labyrinth."

"I thought that was where the children were." She looked at Tim and Grump. "Thank you, Tim, for saving my son's life. I never thought one so young could be so kind and brave."

Tim felt tears filling up his eyes. "You know, Mama G, that Molly and I would do anything for you now. We're like family, and you protect your family whatever the cost."

"Kind, brave and wise," said Thorn. "It is a very good mixture of virtues."

"Are we going to chit-chat like old ladies at a tea party or are we going to go back to the battle?" Grug asked impatiently. "Now that we are winning, I feel like beating some of these huge spiders' bums into oblivion."

"Grug!" Mama G shouted, horrified.

Grump laughed.

*

Lady Sabine didn't have to follow the dark corridors of the labyrinth. Being a spider, she just climbed up the walls and was now jumping from wall to wall towards its centre. Molly sat comfortably on her back. The other spiders followed. They were approaching the centre of the labyrinth and Molly still didn't know what to do when she stood face to face with the Illusionist. She was hoping the answer would just come to her at the right moment. Rooky was nestled comfortably underneath her cloak, his tiny body pressed hard against Molly's heart. They approached the centre of the labyrinth. It was a large space filled with a comfortable armchair, a desk and many chests. But, disappointingly, the centre of the labyrinth was empty.

"Where is she?" Molly asked, her voice racked with frustration.

"I don't know," Lady Sabine said. "She can't be far. We'd better have a good look around."

All the spiders sprawled towards different corridors leading off from the centre. Molly and Lady Sabine stayed put in the middle. Then, suddenly, a cloud of black ravens filled the space from above. They seemed to have come from nowhere. They circled around the spiders and started to throw little pouches at them. Pink mist exploded all around them.

"Don't breathe!" Molly shouted, and she added to Rooky, "Stay where you are!" She put her cloak around her mouth and nose, and breathed through it.

Lady Sabine, quick as lightning, pulled out a handkerchief made from the same material as Molly's cloak, and pressed it to her nose and mouth as well. The other spiders weren't so fast. When the mist evaporated, they were standing motionless with blank expressions on their faces.

"Oh, no," Molly whispered.

Then they heard a laugh – evil, cold and spine-chilling. The Great Illusionist appeared from one of the corridors. She looked menacing and mad. Her face was pale; her lips red; her eyes had dark circles all around them. She wore a long, black dress with holes in the sleeves. But what was most scary about her was her bald and shiny head. It wouldn't have been so horrible if it wasn't right then in the process of transformation. The ravens were coming back to her head. Some of them hung down in loose strands as hair, but some were still birds, or half-birds and half-hair, in the process of re-attaching themselves. The sight was very unnerving.

"My children," the Illusionist addressed the spiders. "Come to me." All the spiders, one by one, approached her, their eyes empty and blank. "Bind our guests up, so they cannot move or hurt your mother."

All the spiders complied. They moved with such speed that Molly and Lady Sabine couldn't really react to it. Within seconds, Lady Sabine was lying on her side with her legs bound tightly, and Molly was sitting on the floor with a strong and sharp web binding her wrists and ankles. The web was so sharp it cut through Molly's skin, and her blood started to trickle down her hands and into a little pot that was lying on the floor. Molly hadn't noticed it before, but now decided to stay still and not move, letting her blood gather there for whatever the reason was.

"What are you doing? Stop!" Lady Sabine shouted at the spiders. "I'm your queen!"

"You're nobody's queen anymore," the Illusionist answered. "I'm their queen now. You should have died in the hole when I put you there."

"It was you!"

"Of course, naïve princess, did you really think that the spiders of the stone labyrinth want peace?"

"I was hoping for that for many years. There has been enough war and hate."

"Just like I said, naïve princess, you are not fit to rule, and this is why I'm taking this burden from you; I'll gladly take your place. As for you, human child, you have created a great deal of havoc, I must say."

"Why are you doing this?" Molly asked. "You could have come back to the sisters, they would help you."

"The sisters!" the Illusionist spat with hate. "I despise them. When I'm at my full power, the other two will die like the younger one."

She doesn't know about Daloba, Molly thought. *I'd better leave it that way.* "Why are you doing this?" she asked again.

"Well, for the power, of course, nothing else. I'm tired of the Wind whingeing, and tired of being constantly told what to do. Now I will be the queen of the worlds and everybody will worship me, that's much more fun. Power is everything."

"That's not true. Friendship and love are stronger!"

"Are they, little girl? So, if the spiders love their queen so much, why are they listening to me? And where are your friends now? Why are they not trying to save you? Oh, wait, they're probably dead themselves now." She laughed a most horrible laugh.

"It's not fair!" Molly protested.

"Life's not fair, little girl," answered the Illusionist. "Only those that are powerful can win in the end."

"It's not true." Molly's voice was weaker now.

"Well, that's enough time wasted," said the Illusionist. "But know my good will. I'm not entirely cruel, you see. I will dispose of you quickly and painlessly and I'll do it before I plunge your world into Darkness, so you don't have to see my new domain." She laughed again.

Molly knew that the end was approaching. She felt that she had failed everybody. The sisters, the hogmills, Sabine and her spiders; now all of them would die because of her. She thought of Tim, of his happy and trusting face. She didn't know what to do. *Sisters*, she thought, *I'm so lost. I'm sorry I've disappointed you.*

"*You didn't disappoint us, Molly,*" came the answer in Taloba's voice. "*Use your gifts, your body is pulsating with them, listen to your heart.*"

Molly looked down at her hands, at her blood gathering slowly in the cup, and she knew what she had to do. She couldn't do it herself, though. She needed Rooky, but he was tucked safely underneath her cloak. *Rooky*, thought Molly, *how can I communicate with him?*

"*Oh my goodness,*" she suddenly heard Rooky's voice in her head. "*Molly, you are freaking me out! Why can I hear you in my head?*"

"*Rooky, can you hear me?*"

"*Loud and clear,*" answered the bird, spooked. "*But how?*"

"*It doesn't matter how, Rooky. Just listen; I know what we have to do. Could you quietly get down towards my hands without her seeing you?*"

The Great Illusionist approached one of the chests and propped it open.

"*I think I can do that, Molly, but why?*"

"*Do you think that the cup my blood is seeping into would be too heavy for you to lift up?*"

"*I don't know, Molly. I can try.*"

The Great Illusionist took out a long and slightly rusty knife from the chest.

"*Then please lift it up and empty it on her head.*"

"*I will try, but I won't stand a chance if she spots me.*"

"*I can hear you too, Molly.*" It was Sabine's voice. "*Let me help you. I'll create a diversion, then you, Rooky, fly like you've never flown before.*"

Now, knife in hand, the Great Illusionist approached Molly.

"*Thank you, Sabine. Thank you, Rooky,*" Molly thought. "*Good luck to all of us. I love you.*"

The Great Illusionist reached her hand out towards her, and Molly closed her eyes. Suddenly she could hear a commotion. She flung her eyes open. Sabine leapt up in the air on her bound legs and rolled onto her side. She was rolling away towards the corridor, making a big noise as she did so.

The Illusionist followed her with her gaze. "Incy wincy jumpy spider!" she said, and followed Sabine. "Maybe you should be the first one to go!"

Rooky got to the cup. It was heavier than he thought. He used all the strength that he had in his little body to lift it up. With difficulty, he gathered height and dropped all the blood on the Illusionist's head. What happened next was truly terrifying. Molly's blood was like acid on the Illusionist's skin – it burnt and sizzled. The Great Illusionist began to scream, and she fell to the floor. Rooky flew back to Molly and freed her wrists and ankles. Then together they crawled to Sabine to free her.

"What's happening to her?" Rooky asked, bewildered.

"I don't know," said Molly, "but it's horrible and I wish it would stop."

And just then the sizzling stopped. One by one, all the hairs started to fall off the Illusionist's head. And as they fell, they became little ravens. They scattered around, stunned.

"My brothers and sisters," Rooky shouted, and flew to them. Their reunion was heart-warming.

The Illusionist lay motionless on the ground. Molly stood up and walked towards the spiders. They stood as if hypnotised, looking at the body crumpled on the floor. Molly started to sing, and touched each and every spider on the head. They shook their bodies until they were fully revived. They ran to Lady Sabine, asking for forgiveness, but she just embraced them, happy that they were back.

"Thank you, Molly," she said.

"Molly, do you mind if we fly and check on our mother?" Rooky asked shyly.

"Of course," said Molly. "Go and check on everybody and tell them that we are fine."

All the birds bowed their heads and took off.

Molly looked down at the Illusionist. "What are we going to do with her?" she asked, wondering.

*

The battle had finished some time ago. All the friends were tired but happy. The spiders of the seventh circle were just finishing locking the prisoners up.

"What are we going to do with all those spiders?" Grump asked.

"We'll wait for Lady Sabine," said Thorn. "She'll talk to their commander, and if I know her she'll try to build a peaceful future for all of our sakes."

"That's the best thing that can come out of it," Mama G said, smiling.

"OK, now I'm seriously hungry," said Grug. "I'm off to find some food and if anybody tries to stop me, remember – I'm a spider rider and a great warrior. You don't want to have another war on your hands."

"I'll go with you," said Arrow with a smile. "Let's get some food for everybody."

Within minutes they were back bringing bags of food from the nearby supermarket.

"Oh my goodness, you won't believe it!" Grug couldn't contain his excitement. "They have a great food house, with only food in it, nothing else."

Grump looked at him, bewildered, and Tim burst out laughing.

"Don't you know about shops?" he said.

"I've heard about them," Mama G said happily, "but I've never seen one."

"Really?" Tim couldn't believe it. "How do you get your food, then? I can give you a guided tour, if you'd like," he joked.

"We grow our own food. Everybody in our tribe has some skill and talent, and we share them for the good of the community. As for a guided tour, that would be very nice, Tim, thank you," she said to Tim's astonishment. "Let us eat first, though."

They didn't have to be told twice. Everybody sat as comfortably as they could on the ground and looked into the shopping bags. They opened all the packets of food and dug in.

Alithema was going through a nice packet of bacon when suddenly Mama G pulled the binoculars out of her bag and put them to her eyes.

"There is a black cloud fast approaching. It looks slightly out of place, I must say."

Everybody stopped eating and looked up.

"Let me fly out and investigate," Alithema mumbled with her mouth full.

"Just be careful, dear," said Mama G. "We don't know what other enemies might await us."

"Yes, ma'am," Alithema said joyfully, and took off. She started slowly, and then suddenly she cried out as if in pain and sped through the air.

Everybody stopped eating and stood up, looking at the departing Alithema with worry on their faces.

"Mama G, what's going on?" Grump asked with uncertainty.

"Have a look yourself," Mama G answered. There were tears in her eyes as she passed the binoculars to Grump.

"Mama G?" Grug started. "Grump, what is it?"

"It's her children!" Grump whispered in a choked voice. "She's got her children back."

They all looked in amazement at what happened when Alithema reached the cloud of birds. They merged together, creating an amazing shape of a magnificent raven. They were like one body, balanced in flight, and each manoeuvre was like a choreographed dance routine. They flew through the sky, rising and falling in unison. They turned circles in the air and whooshed like the wind above the gathered friends, who welcomed such a reunion with cries of joy. Then, tired, all the birds joined the rest of the company.

"These are my children," Alithema said with pride. "All of them, even Rooky, are back."

"Rooky, how is Molly?" Tim asked.

"She was all right when we left her," Rooky answered, "but I'm not sure what's going on there now."

"Tell us everything, please," asked Mama G, and they all listened in suspense.

*

Molly bent over the Illusionist. She didn't look powerful anymore. She was crumpled on the floor, looking vulnerable and sad. Their gazes met.

"Power is the greatest illusion of them all," Molly said with sadness. "I'm sorry it had to come to this."

"You are wrong," the Illusionist whispered back, and then she added something, so quietly Molly couldn't hear it at all.

Then Molly touched her gently on the forehead, put her hands on both sides of her face and started her song. A spiral of dark smoke left the Illusionist's body, and Molly felt that she was holding an ordinary woman in her arms. The woman looked at her, smiled and crumbled to the ground, reduced to ashes. Molly stood up, stretched her arms and absorbed into herself the dark mass floating above her head. When it was done, she fell to her knees and breathed heavily.

"Are you all right, Molly?" Lady Sabine asked with worry in her voice.

"Just tired," was all Molly answered.

"Let's go back to your friends," said the spiders' queen. She helped Molly up onto her back and they left the labyrinth. They managed to find the portal without any problem and, joined by the guardians left there by Thorn, they went through to the human world.

*

Tim was so happy for Alithema. He was so glad they were all alive and that soon it would all be over. He heard a distant drumming.

Thorn's face lit up. "Lady Sabine has arrived in your world," he announced.

"Is Molly with her?" Tim asked, concerned.

"Yes, she is," said Mama G with her binoculars on her nose.

They all waited in suspense. Lady Sabine was approaching them with dignity, surrounded by her spiders. Molly was hunched forward on her back; she looked so small in comparison and really unwell.

"Molly!" cried Tim; he ran to meet his friend and helped her down from Lady Sabine's back. She was so weak he had to support her. Her skin was white, almost transparent, and her hair was thinned out. The friends looked at her in horror.

"She became like that when she absorbed the Darkness into herself," Lady Sabine said with sadness.

"Oh no!" Mama G cried. "The Darkness is consuming her! Molly!" she addressed the girl. "You have to fight it!"

Tim was holding Molly up when she lifted her head and looked at them all. They weren't Molly's eyes looking at them. They were the eyes of the Great Illusionist.

"Tim, move away from her!" Grump shouted, concerned. "She is not Molly anymore!"

"What are you talking about, Grump?" said Tim tearfully. "I don't understand. Of course she's Molly, she's just a little tired, that's all. Molly, tell them it's you. Tell them, Molly."

Molly looked at him and there was such emptiness in her eyes, such an abyss, that Tim could see his friend slipping away from him and disappearing forever.

"Molly!" he pleaded.

"Power!" said Molly weakly in the Illusionist's voice. "It's all that matters. It doesn't matter what body I am in, power can be obtained from anybody." And she laughed, weakly to begin with, but getting stronger and stronger with each passing second.

"Tim! Get away from her!" Grump shouted, horrified.

"No!" Tim shouted back, and the Illusionist laughed. "I won't leave her! Molly is still somewhere there, I know it. She's done this to save us all, she's risked everything, and we can't abandon her now! Molly, please," he pleaded.

Just then, Molly grabbed Tim's arm and dug her fingernails through his skin. "Stupid boy!" she hissed.

"Quickly!" Mama G shouted. "We have to overpower her! Be gentle!" she added.

"Take that rope!" Lady Sabine said quickly, weaving a strong, silky line. "It will hold her tight."

They all ran to Tim's aid and within seconds Molly sat on the ground, securely bound with the silky web. "Stupid creatures!" The Illusionist was furious. "Do you think you can keep me here forever?!" She looked at Tim, and finally Molly's voice broke through: "Tim, help me. Don't let them hurt me. You're my only friend."

Grump grabbed Tim's arms at the last moment before he reached out for Molly.

"It's not her, Tim," he said gently. "She will try every single illusion to trick us into letting her go. We can't let that happen, for Molly's sake and the sake of all the worlds there are."

"What shall we do?" sobbed Tim.

"You can let us past. We can deal with it," said a voice from behind them. Startled, they all looked in the direction the voice had come from. Three women were standing behind them.

"The sisters," Alithema whispered with new hope in her voice.

"The sisters…" everybody repeated with respect and wonder.

Lady Sabine dropped a deep curtsy and all the spiders followed. Mama G bowed her head, but Tim and Grump just stared with their mouths open. Nem and Rod roared and lay on their backs exposing their tummies; the most vulnerable place there is on a tree dragon's body.

"Please, help her," Tim begged through his tears.

"That's why we are here, Tim," Daloba answered, and touched her hand gently on Tim's face. He had felt devastated just moments before, but now he felt strong and able again.

The sisters approached the Illusionist. "You!" she spat, looking at Daloba. "You're supposed to be dead!"

The sisters didn't answer. Taloba approached the Illusionist, took out a little crystal bottle and emptied its contents on her head. She cut the Illusionist free of the web binding her. While she was pouring the contents of the crystal bottle on the Illusionist, Laloba started to sing. It was a song of such immense power that all of the friends were filled with love and creation at the same time. They took hold of each other's hands and stood around the sisters and Molly in a protective circle. The Illusionist screamed in such an agonising voice they all felt pity for her and all their anger towards her left them. The Illusionist's voice changed into Molly's own. They could see the Darkness leaving her body in the shape of black smoke, which was being absorbed into the seed Molly held in her hand.

"Thank you, Molly, for looking after my Seed of Darkness," Daloba said gently. "It is time to give it back now."

"Such a power," said Molly. "Such a power, I can't."

"Molly, give her the seed back." Tim broke the circle and approached his friend. He cupped her face gently in his hands. "Give it back, and let's go back home."

Molly looked at him. "Tim?" she asked. "Is that really you?"

"Of course it's me. Please give the Darkness back. You don't need it."

"I don't want the power of Darkness. The Illusionist made me think that this was what I wanted. She showed me all these pictures in my head. I wasn't sure what was real anymore."

"We are real," said Tim. "Look, we are all here. We are your friends."

Molly looked around at all the familiar faces: Alithema, surrounded by her children; Mama G with her boys; Nem and Rod; and all the spiders; and Tim, her best friend, Tim; all here for her.

"Please, Daloba, take that Darkness away from me. I don't need it." And Daloba took back the Seed of Darkness.

*

"I'm going to miss them so much," Grug said sadly.

They were travelling home on their dragons, Mama G in front of them, singing quietly to herself. She was as upset as the boys when she had to say goodbye to the children. But for the sake of the balance in the worlds, everybody had to get back to their own dimensions. Alithema flew with her children to find a new home. She promised to stay near the hogmills and visit often. Lady Sabine and Thorn were portalled by the sisters to the lands of the seventh circle. They took the prisoners with them and promised to arrange the peace from the safety of their own quarters. The sisters portalled the children, and then went back to wherever the sisters dwelled – although nobody knew where that was. Whatever the future held, they were all part of an extended family now – all bound by the secret of the Underland. The children promised never to mention it to anybody, and anyway, even if they did, who would have believed them?

"I wouldn't worry too much, Grug," said Grump with a mysterious smile.

"What do you mean?" his brother asked.

"I gave Tim my traveller's secret message kit so he can receive messages from us."

"Nicely done," said Grug with a smile.

Epilogue

Timber woke with a nagging feeling that there was something important that he should have remembered, but he couldn't think what it was. He looked up at the window and felt the rays of the sun cascading through the glass straight onto his face. He felt a little bit tired but generally happy. It was a lovely September morning and he had just started Year 5 in his new school. At the beginning of the summer he'd moved with his parents to a new house in a new city. His dad got a new job at the local university and his mum had just opened a new hairdressing salon. He'd been worried about how the move would go, but he really liked his new room in the new house, and the boys at school were much nicer than the boys in his old one. The girls were nicer too. Everything seemed to be much nicer here. His parents were very excited about the move and they seemed to enjoy the new place as much as he did.

Tim jumped out of bed and went to the bathroom to brush his teeth and comb his hair, which was a very difficult thing to do because his hair had always had a life of its own. It stuck out in places and no matter what he did, it always looked like he'd just got out of bed. It was slightly curly, and Tim always thought he could lose a lot of toys in its midst. It actually happened once that he was walking around with two pencils hidden in his hair... it was two days before he discovered them during his weekly hair-washing session. His mum loved his hair, and she was the only person who could just about get it under control. And so she did, when Tim appeared for breakfast.

"How is my favourite boy today?" she asked with a smile.

"I'm fine," yawned Tim into his bowl of cornflakes. "Where's Dad?"

"He had to go to work early today to prepare himself before the students come back for the new term, and there was some trouble in the lab during the night which he's got to sort out."

"What trouble?" asked Tim curiously.

"I don't know; but I'm sure he'll tell us when he comes home. Now, eat your cereal or you'll be late for school," his mum said firmly before leaving the kitchen to finish getting ready for work. "Do you need a lift to school?" she called from the hall.

"No, thanks. I'll walk."

"OK; see you later, sweetheart. I love you," she called as she walked upstairs.

Tim enjoyed the freedom of walking to school all by himself. It made him feel older and more responsible. Just old enough to suit his name – Timber; his mum invented it and he absolutely detested it. He was grateful he could shorten it to something normal! He'd had a lot of trouble with boys at his old school because of his wretched name, and he quickly got used to introducing himself as Tim instead. He didn't mind his new friends calling him that. He didn't mind it because they didn't do it in a nasty manner like the boys from his old school. But now he just wanted to forget about his old life. It was a difficult and not very pleasant one. He had a chance for a new start now and he was planning to grab that chance with both hands.

It was a beautiful September morning. Tim could feel the warmth of the sun on his back as he walked the picturesque route to school. He only had to cross one road and it wasn't a very busy one. He noticed the leaves delicately falling from their branches. He caught a red one and lifted it to the sun. The wonderful red glow softly touched his eyes. He closed them and imagined that he was the captain of a big spaceship flying into space. He and his crew were exploring new ways to travel and he was well known and loved by everybody, and—

"Hi, what are you doing?" A girl's voice brought him back from the sky and he opened his eyes.

"Molly!" he shouted and they both ran towards each other.

"I was worried it was all a dream," said Molly. "I woke up in my own bed, like always, but when I was getting ready I noticed the marks on my arm and everything came back to me. I couldn't wait to see you to check if you'd remembered. When I saw you with the leaf, it was the same as the first time we met, and I was worried that you had forgotten me."

"I hadn't remembered anything," said Tim sadly. "Not until just now… your voice brought it all back to me. You are my lucky charm, Molly." He laughed. "How come we are back to where we started?"

"I think the sisters portalled us back in time, to before our parents went all weird, and before I went missing."

"That's good, at least your parents won't have to worry about you so much. And if I remember correctly, I'm going to be invited to a birthday party I missed the first time round," said Tim with a cheeky smile.

"Ha, ha, ha, that's true. You are certainly invited again." Molly's face changed, her wide smile replaced by a much more sombre expression. "Tim, what are we going to do now?"

"Well, first things first, we have to go to school. I guess we'll settle down into our old lives and find a way to contact Grug and Grump. And of course we'll stay best friends for life; that's what we'll do," Tim said confidently.

"Pinkie promise?" Molly asked with a smile.

"Pinkie promise!" Tim laughed out loud. He grabbed her hand and, with big smiles on their faces, Tim and Molly walked into school together.

Authors Note

The character of Laloba is based on the American legend of bone people. I came across it whilst reading about the wild woman in the book by Clarissa Pinkola Estes, Women who run with the wolves: contacting the power of the Wild Woman, Rider, London 2008.